Crossroads

Also by Steve Jacobs

Light in a Stark Age (Ravan Press)
Diary of an Exile (Ad Donker)
Under the Lion (Ad Donker, Heinemann)
The Enemy Within (Heinemann)

Steve Jacobs

Crossroads

For Yvonne

Crossroads
ISBN 978 1 76041 822 9
Copyright © text Steve Jacobs 2019

First published 2019 by
GINNINDERRA PRESS
PO Box 3461 Port Adelaide 5015
www.ginninderrapress.com.au

Contents

Glossary

ag: expression of irritation

amandla: power, an anti-apartheid rallying cry

aap: ape or monkey

baas: boss

boerewors: type of South African sausage

bakkie: light truck, ute

Boer: farmer, also an Afrikaner

Casspir: armoured personnel carrier

die man is mal: the man is mad

Die Stem: South Africa's national anthem during apartheid

dit is 'n aap: it's a monkey

doek: headscarf

dominee: cleric

ek kom: I am coming

F.W.: President F.W. De Klerk

Hippo: armoured personnel carrier

Inkatha: Zulu political movement, co-opted by and allied with the apartheid government

ja: yes

jou moer: obscene form of address

kierie, knobkerrie: a wooden club

kom, my hond: come, my dog

muti: traditional medicine

naartjie: mandarin, the fruit

nee, mevrou: no, madam

rand: South Africa's currency, hence 'A-rand-a-bag'

ou swaer: literally brother-in-law, but also used informlly as a greeting like 'old mate'.

tsotsi: young street thug

UDF: United Democratic Front, an anti-apartheid movement

Uitlander: foreigner or outsider

vang hom: catch him

voetsek: bugger off

wag net 'n bietjie: wait a moment

witdoek: black vigilantes, co-opted and armed by the apartheid government to force ANC sympathisers from their shacks; they wore white armbands or headbands

A Day in the Life

'Do you have a play by Shakespeare?'

I looked up reluctantly from my crossword. 'Which one?'

'*William* Shakespeare,' she said, rather awkwardly.

'Of course,' I murmured, rising to help. As I led her into the shop, I felt her eyes on my back, unsure whether to trust this guide into a foreign territory. Her suspicion proved well-founded because I abandoned her in the drama section and returned to the safety of my newspaper and coffee. From the desk, I could see her, balanced on high heels before a shelf of titles that she contemplated with obvious and growing confusion, reluctant to touch. In one of the aisles, the vacuum cleaner droned, rotund dog on its morning walk: cleaning is a noisy business and Primrose makes the most of it.

A hand slapped down fifty cents and snatched a *Cape Times*. Quick eyes flashed in a face that was a map of knobs and scars, underlined by a grey wisp of beard. Before I could say good morning, Gibson had gone. I watched him weaving his way through the traffic, a small energetic figure protected from the cold by his balaclava of yellow, green and black stripes. I imagined him leaning against the wall of the Shell garage next door, flipping through the newspaper that he'd bought for Morris as he does every day.

The morning's headlines made me shudder: CROSSROADS DEATH TOLL RISES. I felt that we were at war.

'How are things out your way?' I asked.

Primrose looked up from inside a cloud of dust. 'Only Crossroads is burning,' she said. 'Khayelitsha is quiet.' She returned to her work, green feathers twitching indignantly at dirt trapped between pockets of books.

Overcome by Shakespeare, the woman in high heels hurried out, signalling to me with a shrug that she had given up. I smiled sympathetically and settled down to wait for the housewives and tourists, although there have not been too many of those since the unrest began.

I know I should have been more solicitous, should have tried to clinch the sale, but my mind was not on my job; the great unease in the world had me off-balance. I told myself that she wasn't going to buy anything anyway: she'd strayed in from the beauty salon down the road on a whim, trying to track down a memory from her schooldays.

Two coloured teenagers erupted into the shop, pushing a supermarket trolley full of boxes. '*Naartjies!*' they chimed in unison. '*A-rand-a-bag!* Sweet as honey, more for your money!' They jostled each other in the exuberance of selling.

'They're good for the heart,' the bigger boy declared. The other one nodded sagely, a wide-toothed comb protruding from his head of tight curls like a tipsy halo.

'Tomorrow we got apples,' they promised, and left, nudging and kicking each other around the wheels of the trolley.

When Brian returned from depositing our small profit, I tidied the shelves. I have a theory that the books go visiting at night after we've closed the doors: Conrad had journeyed to the African section to see how Kurtz was doing; Coetzee had left the austere heart of the country for the cooking section, settling between *Scrumptious Cheeseakes* and *1000 Ways with Brown Rice*. A bluebottle, brilliant as an emerald, had chosen to die on the Penguin edition of Kafka's short stories.

Brian, balding and paunchy, a cigarette hanging from his lower lip, was sitting at the desk. The phone rang and he spoke into it, exhaling smoke. 'No, I don't have one in stock at the moment but I can order it from Jo'burg. It'll take two weeks. Fine, I'll call you when it arrives,' he said.

'If lung cancer doesn't get you first,' I muttered, but he waved my comment away with a flick of the wrist. His bracelet tinkled.

At twelve-thirty p.m., a sweating black man in blue overalls delivered *The Argus*. As the pile of papers thudded onto the counter, the headlines screamed: SHACKS RAZED AS MEN GO ON RAMPAGE. Primrose clicked her tongue when she read the report, and shook her head. I took a mouthful of coffee, but it was cold.

During lunch we had a flurry of customers, men buying thrillers and detective stories, and women asking for books of 'nice poems'. They blurred in my mind, became one Secretary selecting Patience Strong and one Chartered Accountant paying for Robert Ludlum.

Brian took his half-hour break after lunch, and I could breathe again. With the vindictiveness of a passive smoker, I threw the ashtray containing his burnt-out ends into the dirt bin. Emotion expended, I stared out of the window. The shop was empty. A few black women from the supermarket next door, done up in bonnets and aprons, were taking their afternoon stroll, pretending to be English country maidens; a white girl, thin as paper, jogged by jerkily, her pained grey eyes reflecting pleasures of bodily torment that slobs like me have been fortunate enough to avoid; the chemist's messenger wobbled his scooter into the traffic, as heavy as the overloaded black taxis that pluck their fares from under the noses of oncoming buses. Across the road, a fat couple squeezed through the turnstiles of the delicatessen, perhaps salivating in anticipation of the smoked salmon on rye which is my favourite.

I was dreaming of Rita when a woman in a blue outfit confronted me, her low neckline revealing a full bosom. I caught a whiff of a rich scent; a diamond put the seal on her pedigree.

'I'm from the Hydrangea Book Club,' she announced with a sweet smile. 'Can you help me with the new books?'

Where was Brian? Book clubs are his department. He loves escorting these bejewelled, thickly made-up wives through the softly erotic delights of the Judith Krantzes and Shirley Conrans: something to do with his mother – we've discussed it.

I looked around frantically, but there was no sign of my partner. And so, fixing a grin on my face, I led her to the hardcover fiction section, where the shelves groaned under the weight of thousands of pages of literature's lucrative flip side, our bread and butter.

She followed me happily, her face bright with anticipation. I felt her heavy warmth, and, despite my strongest efforts, found that I was glancing down the front of her dress. Thankfully, we reached our destination before I could embarrass myself and bring the firm into disrepute.

At random, I started pulling out volumes. 'The new Robin Cook, a medical thriller…and you could try this one about the Arab–Israeli conflict…here's a nice family saga…and this is the latest Stephen King: horror.'

Her gold earrings swung as she leaned forward; her gold necklace tied her domestically to a devoted husband who was a doctor having an affair with his nurse, or a lawyer with his clerk. 'Some of the girls like horror,' she said coquettishly.

'It's very good,' I lied. The husband had better secure that necklace tightly.

'Is it new?'

'These are all new.'

'Which have the other book clubs bought?'

As I floundered for an answer, God showed His mercy: Brian returned. Gracefully, I bowed out. 'My partner will help you,' I said with relief, and left her groping for meaning in a treacherous forest of blurbs, her small mouth twisted in concentration as she tripped over superlatives.

Our bread and butter.

During my break, I walked past Morris's Garage.

Gibson, neat in his blue and red Shell outfit, pulled himself away from the wall beside the cashier's kiosk and sauntered out to meet me. Dreadlocks escaped like eels from under his balaclava. 'Hello,' he rasped. 'Has the new *Learn and Teach* come in yet?'

A team of municipal workers digging up the pavement, watched over by a white foreman, glanced up at Gibson's voice, which grated through the air like a file through bars.

'Not yet. I'll let you know.'

'Thanks.' He stood, looking towards the mountain, his hands thrust deeply into his pockets.

'Excuse me,' I said, self-conscious under the scrutiny of the foreman, 'I have some shopping to do.'

Gibson did not seem to hear, but continued staring at Lion's Head as if the vision of the mountain were the most wonderful sight in the world.

Primrose passed me on her way back from the post office, a pile of parcels in her stately grasp. 'I'm going home now,' she said. 'I must take the early bus…just in case there's some trouble.'

'All right,' I replied absently, still thinking about Gibson. 'I'll see you tomorrow.'

The sun shone brightly, the pigeons foraged in the middle of the road in denial of the danger from traffic, a yellow police van hurtled helter-skelter down the street. I returned to the shop burdened with my bags from Woolworths.

At four-thiry p.m., a harassed deliveryman dropped off the late final. Brian was making tea. I'd served a young couple who were emigrating and wanted a glossy book on Cape Town to take overseas, to remind them, as they put it, 'of this beautiful land'.

Gibson sidled into the shop. He stood at the doorway, squinting at the newspaper. 'It's terrible,' he declared. He did not look at me: he might have been on a platform addressing an audience. 'Last night they burned down my house.'

I inspected the shop anxiously, relieved that there were no other customers.

Gibson jerked his head. 'They chased us away and burned down my house. We just had to run, my wife and my children and me.'

'Who burned down your house?' I asked.

'The *witdoeke*.' His hands groped for imaginary weapons, fended off attackers who lived in his mind.

'Who are these *witdoeke*?' I asked. 'I've read about them in the papers.'

'They live in Crossroads,' he said. 'They want our land. They wear white,' he made a ring around his forehead with a grease-stained finger, '*doeke* on their heads.'

'But what about the police? Don't they help you?'

'The police are there all the time in their Hippos. But they shoot at *us*.' He stubbed his finger on the newspaper. 'They shoot while the *witdoeke* burn our houses. We're their enemy because we give shelter to the comrades when the police are chasing them.'

I stared at him, trying to grasp fully what he was saying.

'The *witdoeke* are like Judas – they betray their own people,' he rasped. 'The government gives them guns and money to attack their brothers and burn down their houses. They get our land and the comrades have no place to hide: that's the deal. But we will have revenge.' He looked up at the ceiling. 'God will help us.'

'Where's your family now? Are they all right?'

He snorted. 'They're staying with my brother in Guguletu. But he's already got fifteen people in his house. It's too small.'

'How do you still manage to come to work?' I asked.

'I must come to work. Otherwise Morris will get someone else in my place. And then how will my family eat? And I must have money to buy zinc…to build my house again.'

He turned to go, but stopped, scratching his head under his balaclava, as if he had forgotten something. He wiped his hand across his eyes. Then he said bitterly, a slight lowering in pitch of the rasp. '*He* doesn't know how difficult it is for me just to come to work.'

Suddenly I blurted out, 'Do you want me to give you a lift home tonight?' The words had a momentum of their own; they escaped from my mouth as fleet and sharp as weasels, surprising me, although he seemed to take my offer for granted.

'The Airport Road is too dangerous,' he said, 'and so is Landsdowne Road. And so is Klipfontein Road. And there are police roadblocks and you can't get through.'

I expected him to thank me, and was piqued when he did not.

'I'll take a taxi,' he said. He dug in his pocket and produced forty cents. 'For *The Argus*.'

'No, keep the money.' Rita would have accused me of being patronising, but Gibson seemed to appreciate the gesture.

He looked directly at me, as if only then discovering that I was present. His teeth were brilliantly white when he smiled. 'Thank you, comrade.'

'A pleasure,' I stammered.

He folded the newspaper under his arm and walked out, chin held high.

For a long time, I stared down the empty aisle at the large Penguin that hugs the wall at the end of the shop; a modern hieroglyph which, to me, represents knowledge, the best face of a flawed mankind.

I was roused from my reverie by an insistent little woman with a beak-like nose and a black moustache. 'Are you serving?' she clucked irritably, stabbing her umbrella into the carpet. 'I'm looking for a bridge book.'

'This way,' I said brusquely, and she waddled after me to the section on card games where I left her.

Brian came out of his office. 'We didn't do so well today.'

'Too bad!' I snapped and he stared at me, taken aback.

He didn't accuse me directly of not doing my job properly but I could see the disappointment in his eyes.

'My, my, we're touchy,' he commented after a while, stroking his mouth for comfort. 'Are we having trouble with Rita?'

'It's nothing.'

'This should cheer you up.' With the flourish of a magician, he produced an envelope from the papers he carried. 'Go on. Open it.'

I did, to humour him. It was already open: he wanted me to repeat an action that must have given him immense pleasure. And I could see why. It was a cheque for more than eight thousand rand for books we had supplied to the government for black education. Brian's face opened up, wide with joy and the expectation of my delight.

'Very nice,' I said, but my happiness was tempered by the disquiet that had settled on me like a Cape winter. Brian took the cheque back without comment, although I could see he was puzzled.

For a moment, we stood in silence, looking past each other like strangers. Through the window, I could see the flower seller sitting despondently outside the delicatessen. A man in a dark blue suit got out of a BMW and bought a bunch of roses from her. She smiled tiredly as she accepted his money; he was smiling, too, as he drove away.

Behind me, the woman carrying the umbrella slapped a book on the counter. 'I'll take this one,' I heard her say.

Brian rang up the sale.

Night settled heavily on the grey city; street lights and car lights tried to ward off the gathering darkness. I pulled a copy of *The Argus* towards me. On the front page was a photograph of the squatter camp, a pall of smoke hanging over it like a volcanic cloud. With morbid fascination, I read the accompanying article. It began, 'The body lay on its back at the side of the road, charred beyond recognition – a victim of the Crossroads strife…'

*

A fifty-cent coin drops on the counter and I look up. It's Morris.

'Where's Gibson?' I ask as he takes a *Cape Times* with dirty fingers. 'I haven't seen him lately.'

Morris shakes his head; he has sad eyes. 'The bugger didn't come to work, so I had to let him go. You just can't trust them these days, can you? He hitches up his pants and shuffles out, muttering, 'You can't trust them at all…'

From the street, a voice chimes, '*A-rand-a-bag! A-rand-a-bag!*'

The rain has started to pelt down – a cold rain that drowns out the mountain and sends the people in the street scurrying for cover.

At Play

'Sometimes I feel that somebody's up there,' Smit said.

Ellis picked at a sore on his chin. 'I know how you feel.'

'No, really!' Smit insisted. 'Somebody.'

'*Ja.* You think about it.'

The van sped over the tarmac. A wall rose up on the passenger's side, on Smit's side, and ran along the length of road; they seemed to be driving in a gulley. The wall had an uneven surface, like that of a cliff face, pocked and ridged. At regular intervals there were cracks where the massive blocks of the structure had been fitted together.

Smit's feet slammed on the floor of the van. 'Hey, watch out!' he yelled.

'All right, I can see,' said Ellis with a hint of impatience. 'It's just bloody difficult to control this thing.'

The van spun around a hillock that stood in its path, like a tooth, on its flat base, the point towards the sky.

'I wish they'd keep the fuckin' streets clean.'

'Just slow down, man, that's all. Then you'll see these things in good time.'

'*Ja,*' said Ellis.

But the van continued at the same pace, swerving around impediments. Long grasses sprouted from fissures in the road and in the adjoining wall, thin blades that repeatedly lashed against the window, threatening to slice where they landed.

Smit was more at risk than the driver; the knife edges brushed past his elbow. 'Listen, man,' he said, trying to keep his voice calm, 'I'm not complaining, but you're driving like a kaffir. I don't mind getting killed for a good reason, but not because of your driving.'

The vehicle stopped abruptly. Both men were slung forward. Smit hit his head on the windscreen, Ellis wrapped around the steering wheel.

'Shit,' Ellis swore. 'It's a bastard to drive.'

Smit fell back into his seat. 'Just as well you braked,' he said. 'You would have hit that.'

A brown mound faced them. Its smooth sides rolled gently upward in curls like a dollop of ice cream, beautifully textured and layered, blocking their way.

'Shit,' repeated Ellis, apparently in shock. 'You only see these things at the last minute.'

'I told you to slow down.'

'My reflexes are good.'

'*Ja*, I suppose so. Just be careful, that's all.'

The police van stood at the roadside. Its green canvas flaps kept the sides concealed, where captives might have looked through the wire mesh. Its body was yellow with blue star-like insignias on the doors of the cabin. Around, the huge vegetation unfurled like umbrellas, spun in giant coils, dwarfed the men and their vehicle.

Ellis was staring straight ahead, deep in thought.

'Did you hear what the okes did?' Smit asked, interrupting his partner's daydream.

Ellis blinked and rubbed his bruised ribs. 'No. What?'

'They were arsing around.'

'They usually do.'

'It was Hennie and Kobus. They were chasing some kaffir kids after a riot.'

'Those two,' Ellis responded without interest. 'They're wild sometimes.'

'*Ja*. They chased those kids into a room and fucked them up.'

'So what?'

'This other kid came in and they fucked him up also.'

'*Ja*? So what?'

'He kept saying he hadn't been in the riot.'

'They all say that.'

'Well, no, it was true, Piet. This kaffir didn't lie. And Hennie and Kobus knew it. But they didn't know what to do with him after they'd fucked him up.'

'So what did they do?' Ellis lit a cigarette and tossed the match out of the window. The wind swirled it away.

'So I told you they were arsing around. So Hennie says, "What must I do with this kaffir?" And Kobus says, just in a joke you know, he says, "Shoot him." So Hennie shot him.'

Ellis snorted. 'Serves the kaffir right.'

'Killed him too. But it was OK. The captain got them off.'

'Good old Hennie and Kobus.'

'Have you heard about Hennie's wife?'

'No. What?'

'They say she's a teaser.' Smit grinned wickedly.

'Who says so?' Ellis bit his nail carefully, pulling it off at the length he intended.

'Oh, all the okes. It's well-known. She tried it with André once.'

'Really.'

'*Ja.*'

The exchange foundered on the rocks of the encroaching night. In the distance, a spill of jacaranda flowers lost its colour to the darkness. The radio crackled meaninglessly; there had been no orders from it for hours.

'You know,' said Smit after a while, 'they really control us up there. It's yes sir and no sir and thank you sir and fuck you sir. And then we come onto the street and we can do what we want. Even kill kaffirs and thieves. It's funny, hey?'

Ellis flicked his cigarette butt out of the window. 'Very funny. Ha ha. *Ja*, of course they control us.'

Somewhere was a rumbling like thunder, or an earthquake, or the passage of huge animals. Neither man commented on the noise.

'That thing stinks,' Smit grumbled, indicating the mound ahead. 'Let's go.'

'*Ja*,' said Ellis.

The police van lurched forward, skipped around the dark hummock of dog shit and moved off rapidly down the road. It took corners on two wheels, whizzing around obstacles that loomed before it and disappeared suddenly.

Smit was ashen, Ellis non-committal. They passed big yellow or brown leaves, thin as dried skins, veined and cracking, supported on stalks or lying on their backs like dead cockroaches.

'Listen, man,' said Smit, 'you're driving this bloody thing too fast.'

'You're a cop. You're not afraid, are you?'

'No, but I'm gonna puke if you don't slow down.'

'We're just arsing around, Lenny. That's all.'

*

The boy picked his way over the sharp pebbles and around the piles of dog shit in the gutter at the roadside; he was barefoot. He had short-cropped blond hair and wore a yellow T-shirt that his dad had brought him back from work. It had a blue police star on the front and the word 'Captain' on the back. He manipulated the remote control box he held in his skilled, feverish fingers.

'Vroom! Vroom!' he growled. 'This is headquarters calling car number 5. Come in car number 5. I want you to go to the corner of Main Street and…and…' The boy tried to think of another street, but could not. 'Vroom!' he repeated. 'Terrorists! Go catch them!'

The toy police van sped away under his guidance. The plastic policemen jerked in their seats and the pieces of green cloth flapped against the vehicle's realistic wire-meshed side.

'Vroom!' the boy urged, hunched forward at play.

*

The radio barked at last. The orders were coming through.

'…I want you to go to the corner of Main Street and…and…'

But the voice petered out and there was only static.

'And what, headquarters?' Ellis demanded. 'Where are we going? I don't know where we're going.'

But all the radio said was, 'Vroom!'

Crossroads

I glanced across the cabin. Jeremy was staring, without seeing, at the road ahead; his spectacles reflected his focus inward. I lit a cigarette with trembling fingers and blew out a cloud of smoke. Jeremy, a non-smoker, did not protest.

At the roadblock, a Buffel armoured personnel carrier hulked under the branches of a blue gum tree, a prehistoric creature, undecided whether to put down its nose and graze amicably, or to attack.

Jeremy stopped the *bakkie*. Two soldiers pulled themselves reluctantly away from their brazier and ventured into the cold to inspect the dark cabin. The mere sight of their uniforms was more chilling than the evening.

My notebook and camera were stuffed under the seat. Jeremy had suggested that I hide them in the woodpile, but I hadn't wanted to risk damaging the camera. Now, I worried. Surely these frozen and bedraggled young men would not unpack the entire trailer load. But under the seat… What if they decided to search the cabin? My eye began to twitch as it does when I'm under pressure.

'We're taking this wood into Nyanga,' Jeremy offered, presenting his letter of authorisation to enter a black area. 'We're relief workers.'

I noticed his politeness because it was so studied, so out of character.

'Can we have some?' one of the soldiers asked. They were still boys.

Jeremy's red fists clenched on the steering wheel in a spasm of anger, but his voice betrayed no emotion. 'Go ahead,' he told the pale, pinched fact at the window, and the soldier nodded in gratitude.

'It's not safe in there,' the boy warned. 'They're mad. They're killing their own people. I don't understand them.'

'We'll take our chances,' Jeremy said.

The pink forehead creased dubiously, then the face moved away.

'Why doesn't the army give you wood?' Jeremy continued rhetorically as the miserable soldiers helped themselves to a few logs. 'You'd think the state would be able to warm you.' He started the engine, and edged the *bakkie* forward into the township.

The shacks of KTC crouched like beaten dogs under the grey Cape winter. Loose sheets of corrugated iron cracked like gunshots in the wind. But Terminus Road was dressed for carnival. Stacks of apples and oranges threatened to spill off crowded trestle table tops; goats' heads, still boasting sharp horns, reprimanded anyone who cared to look into their glazed yellow eyes. Entrails, coated black with flies, hung from wooden posts while mouth-watering smells of cooking meat hauled people out of their shacks to buy. A kiosk advertised SHOE REPAIRS; another sold tinned groceries. People milled everywhere: in the road, between the shacks, buying, selling, watching.

'Looks safe enough to me,' I muttered and Jeremy laughed, a sound like a machine needing oil. Our breath formed pale ghosts in the cabin.

We drove past a square in the squatter camp in which neat rows of shoes, an army of invisible protectors, waited for the order to march off in defence of this barren inheritance.

'Here we are.'

I pulled my camera and notebook from under the seat. Visible above the Vibracrete wall, a cluster of brown tents marked with Red Cross symbols huddled together under the protection of the church steeple.

We entered the open gateway, bouncing into a wide, sandy yard, skirted a pool of water, and were immediately surrounded by a mob of children who leaped, snotty-nosed, on to the trailer, hitching a ride. A few men stood about, wearing blankets or smoking pipes, chafing like caged animals, restless eyes staring out of impassive faces. Women carried babies and cooking pots or filled buckets of water from an outside tap.

'The women have adapted better to the centre than the men,' Jeremy remarked. 'They get on with running the place… The men are waiting for the next attack.'

I squeezed the shutter release gently. The click sounded disproportionately loud in the still evening air. A Casspir idled by, heavy as a galleon, and, impetuously, I clicked again.

'Be discreet!' Jeremy snapped at me. 'Don't make our job more difficult.'

'Sorry. But you know how it is. My editor will give me hell if I don't bring back pictures.'

Jeremy snorted and opened his door, 'Hello, Iris,' he said.

The big woman had an open, childlike face. Her eyes were round and gentle as a puppy's; her huge breasts could have comforted the whole of Crossroads. They shook hands, a threefold clasp.

'This is Lucas Goddard,' Jeremy introduced me. 'He's writing a story for the paper on the centre.'

Iris smiled, accepting whomever Jeremy brought in. 'Hello, Lucas,' she said.

Her grip was soft, her palms calloused, and I was careful not to crush her fingers as my big hand enclosed hers. A vein throbbed in my temple; it beat out a warning to her: 'Do not trust this man, standing so innocently before you.' But she did not hear it.

'I've brought wood,' Jeremy was saying. 'Can you get someone to offload it?'

Iris half-turned and yelled orders across the yard. Her voice rounded up a flurry of children who fell upon the trailer like a flock of sparrows. 'Where did you get so much?' she asked.

'It was a donation from a pest control business –' Jeremy began but he was interrupted.

Out of nowhere, materialising from the crisp, smoky township air, a teenage boy had appeared. He wore a girl's dress improbably over trousers and a shirt. He fired a rapid burst of Xhosa at Iris, a series of clicks that I regretted I could not understand. He ended his speech with a sharp flourish of his hands, and, as Iris opened her mouth to reply, he set off on a crouching run towards the church, over a well-trampled vegetable garden.

'That boy, Xolo,' Iris explained, whistling slightly through the gap between her front teeth, 'he says that the *witdoeke* are going to attack us again soon. He says I must tell you to take the women and children away from here.' Her wide forehead was creased in a frown.

'And what do you think?' I asked, seizing my chance. 'Will there be another attack?'

Iris nodded vigorously. 'Today two policemen came here with a man. He said that he was looking for his child. But he was a *witdoek*. The police brought him here to spy on us.'

I made a few notes and Iris nodded, satisfied. A small boy had wrapped himself around her legs. She lifted him in her arms, and the child burrowed into her armpit. I reached to pat him on the head, and then recoiled at the patch of angry skin that blazed from his scalp.

Iris saw my reaction. 'Mvusi was hurt when the *witdoeke* burned down his shack,' she said. 'His mother, she died. You must tell that to your newspaper!'

I grimaced. The sickness in my stomach was worsening.

'Come, I'll take you inside,' Jeremy said, combing away the fringe of fair hair that fell over his eyes.

He left his car door open, I closed mine, and we walked towards the building, stepping around puddles and mud patches. The off-loading was continuing with a great deal of enthusiasm and noise.

A thick smell of paraffin and musty cooking clogged up a doorway. A queue of people waited against the brick wall. Some fidgeted, some stood patiently with faraway looks in their eyes. They wore *doeks* and caps, jeans and frocks, a motley selection of second-hand clothes. A baby squalled; another, hearing its protests, added a yelp of its own before it was clutched to a breast.

As we walked, Mvusi peeked over Iris's shoulder at me, a cheeky grin in his big eyes. I smiled back, and took a photograph. The boy quickly buried his head and the wound stared at me like a pink eye.

A bone-thin man was tottering through the mud to meet us. He grabbed Jeremy's shoulder, and held on, swaying like a dilapidated boat at anchor. He wore a red jersey and ill-fitting trousers. 'Hey, Jeremy, man,' he jabbered.

'What is it, Monde?'

'Listen, man, Jeremy…' His eyes were wild. 'I need bus fare…' He stopped, pleading in silence.

'I'm sorry, Monde. We have no money for bus fare. You know that. All our money goes on food and blankets and paraffin. I'm sorry, but we can't help with that sort of thing.'

The thin man shook his head, as if to ward off the distress that would swallow him. Then he peered into Jeremy's face, cunningly. 'Last night I had a dream about a cow. It was crying. It said I must go back to the Transkei. It went, "Mooo!"'

Some children nearby giggled as Monde moaned. 'I must go back to the Transkei,' he begged. 'My nature is all wrong here.' He held up his wrist and a few bangles rattled down into his sleeve. 'That's why I'm so thin. I must kill the ghosts.' He pointed across the wall. 'I need bus fare, man, Jeremy. There's too much trouble here. I must go back to my mother's house.'

Jeremy stared into the mud, his eyes burning with helplessness. 'I'm sorry, Monde,' he said quietly. 'I've told you before.'

The beggar relaxed his grip and stepped back as if he were taking his last look at the stringy, harassed relief worker. 'I love you, man, Jeremy. You're helping us so much.'

'We do our best.'

'Well then, can I have a rand for cigarettes?'

Exasperation put an edge to Jeremy's voice. 'If I give to you, I'll have to give to everyone. There are five hundred people in this centre. That's five hundred rand just for cigarettes.'

'Not everyone,' Monde persisted. 'Not everyone smokes. Just give to me.'

A thin dog slunk past the hungry queue outside the kitchen, head tucked into the space between its legs, studiously ignoring the smell of food.

I slipped my fingers into my pocket and gave the man a rand. Monde pumped my hand gratefully, and I felt the hard outline of the coin in his palm.

'Thank you, thank you, man.' He made to go, and then turned back to me, and tears were streaming down his face. 'My child died in the fighting,' he said, and stumbled away blindly.

'You shouldn't have given him,' Jeremy chided.

'Shit!' I bristled. 'He just wanted a rand. And his child…'

'I've got to work here. You're just visiting. This begging won't help anyone. We *must* guard against dependency. You might salve your conscience for a rand but it won't fix anything.'

My anger ebbed away. 'You know best,' I conceded.

'Let's go.'

A burly man wearing a leather jacket and sunglasses swaggered out of the building. He greeted us with a clenched fist. 'Hello, comrades!' he boomed. His beard hairs were combed out in single strands, electrically straight.

'Comrade,' Jeremy acknowledged, and muttered to me, 'He's the big shot around here. He's quick to criticise when we aren't democratic. But *he* doesn't do anything. *He* doesn't try to help.'

The stifling smell from the crowded kitchen pulled people in from the queue with its thick fingers. Inside, a single low light bulb cast shadows over the feeding of the multitude.

'You see,' Iris said proudly. 'The people are eating.'

Sweaty, tired-ooking women were busy sawing up loaves of bread and smearing jam on to each slice with bent tin lids. One poured soup from huge steaming pots into polystyrene cups. Each pair of hungry hands received a cup of soup and a chunk of bread.

'We've still got enough for two days,' said Iris, pointing to the back wall, where fresh loaves were stacked like bricks together with cartons of tinned foods, some without labels.

As I watched, I could not help but reflect that a few miles away in the white suburbs, comfortable citizens were settling down to their

Sunday evenings: supper, a church service and later a symphony concert on TV. And then, warm beds. Through the single misted window, I could see the sand dune that was the KTC squatter camp. Shanties clung defiantly to its shifting surface. Behind it, belonging to the other world, the world of the whites, was the dim outline, almost lost in cloud and night, of Table Mountain.

Iris opened a door. Lit by candles, an inner sanctum was revealed, a storeroom, where a group of men and women sat on blankets, talking earnestly as the shadows, fuelled by the draught, cavorted, distorting their features. One or two faces looked up and greeted us. I nodded. Iris said something in Xhosa and Jeremy agreed, as though he understood a few words.

'The committee is meeting. Come. We must leave them to their work.'

The heat and smell were making me light-headed and I was relieved to follow my guides back through the kitchen, jostling past the queue. The cold air stung my face and I took a deep breath, inhaling the smell of wood smoke, savouring the chill of the evening. The trailer shone, oily with dew, stripped of its load by the children.

'Do any of the people here plan to move out to Khayelitsha as the government wants?' I asked Iris.

'We want our old land back, that they've chased us off, so we can build our houses again,' she said. Mvusi twitched in her arms.

'And if you don't get it back?'

Iris shrugged, and a sad smile softened the tension in her face. 'There's going to be more fighting,' she said, jabbing her forefinger towards the street. 'At night, an ambulance drives around here. It has black crosses on the doors. We think there are policemen inside. Or soldiers. And *witdoeke* with guns from the police.'

'If you get the number, we can check it out,' Jeremy said.

'That won't help. They've already decided…' She did not finish.

The howl of an engine and a shrieking of brakes tore into her words as a yellow police Casspir careered around the corner into Terminus

Road. Two orange bursts of flame spurted from its nostrils, followed by a thudding as it champed its jaws together. Without thinking, I found myself galloping towards the wall, caught up in the surge of the refugees' curiosity. By the time I had flung myself against the concrete, the monster had gone. A fusillade of shots rang out somewhere in KTC.

I walked back, dragging my wet heels in frustration at missing the story. I had blundered through mud and water, and the cold was beginning to grip my soaked feet. 'I didn't see who they were shooting at,' I complained.

Jeremy took off his glasses and wiped them. 'Probably some comrades,' he answered. 'Who else?'

Iris was standing in the same spot I had left her; she was comforting Mvusi, who had begun to cry.

'You were saying *they've* decided,' I said, picking up my earlier line of questioning. 'Who's decided what?'

'The police and the soldiers and the *witdoeke*.' Iris was bouncing the child on her hip. 'Today a Casspir came past and the policeman told us in Xhosa. He said we must all go to Khayelitsha because they want to burn down the centres and KTC.'

'I can't see them attacking the churches.'

Iris glanced at me with contempt for not understanding. 'They can do anything.'

Suddenly there was a commotion at the wall; people scattered in all directions as Xolo, the boy in the dress, flung himself into the church grounds and burrowed into one of the tents like a rabbit, emerging seconds later without the dress, just another teenager. Iris was bustling Jeremy and me into the kitchen, into the storeroom, herding us with her free hand, following us in. The room was now empty and dark.

I sucked in breath sharply. My hands, clutching my notebook and camera, were sweating.

'Stay here and be quiet!' Iris ordered. She was breathing shallowly, I could hear, and Mvusi whimpered.

'What's happening?'

Iris opened the door a crack. By the light that streamed in, I saw her chest heaving. 'All I know is the shooting,' she said. 'If they saw Xolo come in here, they'll search. If they find you, they'll say you brought in guns. And there'll be trouble for us.'

'What about the *bakkie*?'

She squeezed her way out. 'It belongs to the dominee's brother.'

'And Xolo?'

'They won't know him without his dress. We all look the same to them.' She laughed bitterly and closed the door. 'Don't leave until I fetch you.'

The blackness was overwhelming. There was nothing else to do but sit on the blankets and wait. In the kitchen, the activity continued as before, belying the tension. The 'ping' of metal punctuated a background noise of muffled voices and shuffling feet.

I rubbed my pen against my cheek. 'What an irony…' I mused. I had not intended to reveal my secret, but now, somehow, secrecy did not matter.

'What is?' Jeremy asked distractedly.

A black wall separated us.

I did not have to tell him, but the conflict that manifested as a sickness in my gut, as an abhorrence for the soldiers' uniforms, needed expression.

'Today I'm hiding from the police,' I said. 'But next week I'll be swapping sides.'

'Swapping sides?' he snapped, now giving me his full attention.

'I've been called up for an army camp.'

Jeremy let out a long sigh. 'Will you go?'

'I don't know.' I sniffed loudly, looked for a handkerchief, but could not find one. 'How can I put on that uniform?'

Talking was not helping. I felt the blood pounding in my head; the smell from the hot kitchen in the airless room stuffed nausea like a gag into my throat. 'I don't want to go to jail or exile.'

'Well, I hope you haven't been posted here,' he said. 'It would be very embarrassing, to say the least, for me if people recognised you. They'd probably fucking kill me. Why didn't you tell me?'

I turned on him then, maddened by his self-righteousness. 'It's easy for you!' I shouted. 'You don't have to go.' I breathed deeply, fighting for air.

'I served my time too,' he said. 'Do you think you're the only one?'

'Don't worry,' I retorted. 'I won't embarrass you. I've been posted to Potchefstroom.' I clutched my pen tightly in the darkness. 'My whole adult working life has been spent exposing the excesses of the government. That's how I serve my country. And now they've called me up for a camp. Out of the blue. Shit!'

Jeremy cleared his throat, but did not speak.

'I love this fucking country. I don't want to leave...'

We sat in silence, hardly able to see each other. After a time measured in deep breaths and heartbeats, the door opened and Iris's head appeared, framed in light.

'Everything's all right,' she said. 'They drove straight past.' But her face was pinched and frowning and her eyes were wet. Tears rolled down her cheeks and she tried to catch them in her fingers, but they dripped through. 'They shot Monde,' she said.

'Oh God, no!' Jeremy dragged his blunt fingers down his face. 'Is he...?'

'Xolo says he's dead. They took his body away with them. He had a gun and he shot a soldier, and they chased him into KTC and they killed him.'

I felt in my pocket, reliving the movement of giving Monde the rand. I could still feel the hard coin digging into the heel of my hand. It had been a last request.

I walked to the car, for a moment forgetting to write, and sat inside. Jeremy got in behind the steering wheel. He looked older, as if crows had perched on his cheeks, raking the skin around his eyes. It was dark by now, and we drove slowly down the road towards the roadblock. The trailer bounced emptily behind us.

Outside Intervention

1. Arrival

A shooting star flashed across the sky. Then another. Soon, the heavens were criss-crossed by streaks of light. All the radios and TV sets went dead and the people in the townships thought it was a police raid. In that brief moment, when silence fell as suddenly as those lights from the sky, you didn't know what was going on and you believed the first thing that came into your head: police, *tsotsis*, mobs to petrol-bomb your house...whatever. Only later, when none of these things happened, when the tear gas did not burn you out into the streets, when the electricity did not return and the delivery vans did not bring bread and milk, when the buses did not come to take the people to work; only then did you begin to understand that things were worse than usual. And when you left your township on foot and walked towards the town or city where you worked, you saw that the roads were deserted. A few cars had stopped on the freeway or had slewed off into the bushes. They were empty. And what you noticed most of all was the silence. No smoke belched from factories, no noise of the city intruded into your early-morning silent world; your greatcoat turned you into a cocoon from which no butterfly might ever emerge.

2. Outside

Wagenaar slumped on the neck of his horse. The animal breathed noisily through its dilated nostrils; its brown hair was stained with sweat after the hard ride.

'Listen, man,' Wagenaar gasped, 'we must stop here. I've had it.'

'Bullshit, brother,' said Patrick Mtetu. 'Bullshit. Get up. Sit up.' He reined in his horse.

Its eyes stared wildly as it fought him for a moment, then surrendered to his will. The two horses stood side by side, pawing at the ground, while the men on their backs decided what to do next.

'It's no use,' Wagenaar whispered. 'Please help me down. Or I'll fall.'

As the black man buckled under the weight of his white companion, Wagenaar moaned. On the ground he gave up the battle against his pain. Mtetu had never seen Wagenaar cry; the bulky man did not shed tears easily.

'Those fucking Martians,' Wagenaar squeezed from between clenched teeth. His face, the part not covered by beard, was deathly white.

'Yes,' Patrick Mtetu responded, as if in refrain. 'Those fucking Martians.'

'Fucking Martians,' Wagenaar repeated. 'Why couldn't they leave us alone?' He breathed quickly and shallowly.

Patrick dragged him, propped him up against a rock.

'I'm going to die. You know that? Those politicians sent us to die. Nothing ever changes, does it? T'n'T: the dynamite twins.'

'You're not going to die, brother. Don't bullshit me, man.'

Wagenaar laughed quietly and winced with the effort. He rested for a moment, then looked around. The veld might become the repository of his bones; enough of his forefathers were buried there. The rolling hills were so gentle: as his eye rested on them, it seemed improbable that they were the impartial witnesses to so much killing.

'Maybe our great-grandfathers fought each other in these hills,' he said. 'Can you imagine that?'

'It's possible,' the black man said. 'Maybe tonight we'll see the ghosts riding on their horses…'

'With herds of cattle across the river. Rifles blasting in the moonlight…'

'We aren't going to be here tonight. You're going to get on your horse so that we can be back at the house by sunset. Do you want Leon and Levin to come looking for us? To risk their lives in the dark because you were too bloody lazy to get back on your horse?'

'Don't talk rubbish. They won't come. Maybe the archbishop will come himself.'

Wagenaar held his hand out, and the other man took it. The white hand was as weak as a doll's; Patrick Mtetu felt that he was holding the hand of a corpse already. The sensation of touching death flowed over him and he had to shake his head because it threatened to gum up his eyes.

Wagenaar did not notice his companion's reaction; he was lost in a world of his own, where the soft pink sunset settling on an olive landscape did not include aliens. In this world, everyone was safe, houses contained families, blacks lived in their own areas, you knew where you stood.

A face melted through the vision and planted itself before his eyes. 'Johan,' the bloodless lips mouthed, 'are you coming now?'

'*Wag net 'n bietjie,*' he said. 'Wait.'

'Johan…'

'I'm coming. They shot me.'

'What's that?' Patrick asked. 'What did you say?' He still held the limp fingers.

'Rika…'

'Is dead,' the black man said. 'Your wife is dead. You know that.'

Wagenaar's fingers suddenly acquired power. They grabbed Mtetu's shirt front and pulled him down. They knew, for an instant, their original power, the power they had possessed that morning, thick farmer's power. Patrick's head snapped down; their foreheads almost collided.

'You lie, kaffir,' Wagenaar whispered and, despite the white man's pain, Mtetu slapped his face.

'Don't ever call me that, you bastard. I'm nobody's kaffir any more. Do you hear me? All that's changed. It's different now. My wife's dead too. And Leon's. And Levin's.' He pulled himself away and felt his shirt (his only one) tear. 'You're nothing special. Stop feeling so sorry for yourself.'

'Rika,' Wagenaar pleaded, 'come back.'

'I should leave you here. Do you know that? I should leave you to the jackals and the hyenas. They'll pick your fucking bones clean. Then you'll know what it's like to be white.'

Mtetu stood up, laughing, and stomped around in the dirt, his boots crunching stones and disturbing lizards. Wagenaar lay where he was, his eyes closed, his empty fingers clutching air. He seemed to be sleeping.

*

A half-moon clawed its way into the black sky. It was white as ice, pocked with flaws. It picked its way between packs of stars and hung like a leer in the primitive darkness.

A small fire flickered patterns on the rocks and the faces of the men who watched it; it crackled and hissed, reminding Patrick Mtetu of the fires that had swept through the township in the days before the aliens came. He watched the tame monster: how quickly could such an infant, left unattended, swell into a snarling adult bent on reducing humans to coals and buildings to black stones. Perhaps the aliens had come just in time. Who could say?

'I'm sorry for what I said this afternoon,' Wagenaar offered suddenly. 'I was dreaming.'

'It's OK.'

'Those fucking Martians. You know, when that shot hit me, I felt the same way as when I used to play rugby and the other bloke tackled me and I was winded. I felt like they had sucked all the wind out of me. And look. There isn't a mark on me anywhere. But, *jislaaik*, those dreams. I dreamed I saw Rika.'

'I know.'

'I dreamed she was calling me to join her.' He shivered. 'It was just her head. Nothing else.'

'How do you feel?'

'OK now. I slept.'

'We'll have to wait for morning. It's too dark to ride now.'

'That's fine with me,' Wagenaar chuckled. His old sparkle had returned. 'Let Leon and Levin worry about us. Maybe I'll recover. I feel better now. Maybe I'm too strong…' But he did not believe what he was saying: once they got you, you were dead; no one recovered. At night, out in the hills, it helped to pretend, to believe. 'Do you think they're chasing us?' he asked.

'They would have caught us by now.'

The farmer closed his eyes. 'Yes, I suppose so.'

'They could fly over and blast us out of sight whenever they wanted.'

'*Ja*,' said Wagenaar. 'Who knows what they're thinking? I wonder what they want with us. Maybe they don't think like we do.'

'What I want to know,' mused Patrick Mtetu, 'is where is the rest of the fucking world.'

'*Ja*.' Wagenaar's tone conveyed his scorn. 'They couldn't keep their bloody noses out of our business with all that apartheid stuff. But as soon as we really need them, there's no one in sight.'

'Maybe South Africa's been cut off, you know. Maybe they've put a shield round us,' Patrick ventured. 'So no one can get in.'

'Why would they want to do that?'

'To get our gold?'

'What would Martians do with gold?'

'The same as us, I suppose.'

'Maybe they're just watching us, like animals in zoos. Maybe that's why they don't just kill us all.'

'Who knows?'

'Maybe they're keeping us like we kept the animals on the farms, you know. And they'll eat us one by one when they're hungry.'

'That's terrible,' Patrick shivered. 'Fuck them.'

There was a long silence, punctured by the breathing of men and horses. It was useless to try to interpret the aliens' motives; it was foolish to imagine that alien logic could be accessible to humans.

Could primitive tribes, invaded by Europeans, understand the reasonings of their new overlords?

Wagenaar broke into Mtetu's thoughts. 'You know,' he said, 'when they shot Rika, I wished they had shot me too. I thought there was no point in going on. But now I want to live. I want to get those bloody *uitlanders* out of my country and I want my farm back. I want to plant more fruit trees and I want to increase my herds.'

'What happened to your workers? When the Martians came.'

'I don't know. They ran away, I suppose. I don't blame them. I also ran. Rika was dead.'

Patrick put his hand on the big Afrikaner's shoulder, comfortingly. 'So did I,' he said. 'We all ran.'

'When we get them out, you must come and visit me on my farm,' Wagenaar said. 'I'll be alone and it gets pretty lonely out there on the stoep at night. It'll be nice to have visitors. You must come and stay. For as long as you want. You hear?'

'Thanks, brother. I'll do that.'

'Africa belongs to Africans, not to those bloody foreigners. They just mustn't mess with my fruit trees…'

'And you must come and see where I live,' Patrick said. 'It's not much, but it's home. There won't be so many people, it won't be so overcrowded as it was. But I'll also be missing my wife and friends. The streets may be empty. Have you ever been to a location?'

'Only to fetch my labourers. And not during the unrest.'

'No more unrest, brother. No more burning, no more violence. The Martians have changed all that. It's a pity we couldn't learn by ourselves. They had to teach us.'

'*Ja.* Fucking Martians,' Wagenaar chuckled. 'It's still apartheid, hey? Things haven't changed for you at all, *ou swaer*. First it's the English and then it's the Afrikaners and now it's the fucking Martians.'

'Now you know what it was like for us. Hiding and running, police everywhere, questions. Tension, brother, tension.'

'Well, it's all over now,' the Afrikaner said. 'Remember. If I die, and you come out alive, go and look after my farm for me. Raise chickens and find a wife and have lots of children…'

'Can I have that in writing? If you die, who'll believe me when I say you gave me your farm?'

The farmer sighed. 'If I had a pencil and paper, I'd write it.'

'Never trust a white man,' said Patrick and they both laughed.

The moon, the lunatic grin in the dark, was at the top of the sky and the fire had died down to embers. Mtetu drank from his water bottle and stared into the valley below as though, if he looked closely enough, he would see the spirits of his ancestors, armed with spears and shields, facing the rifles of the white settlers. Perhaps, one night, years in the future, a descendant of his would be sitting on this very hillside, watching battles between humans and aliens. Did aliens have souls that would come back on certain nights to contend with human spirits in phantom battle? Would he live to produce descendants? Who could know?

Wagenaar sprawled on the damp ground, in the position he had assumed during the evening. Only very soft breathing revealed that he was still alive. Mtetu was reminded of the tramps and the meths drinkers who used to lie in similar postures of total abandon on the streets of the white cities, while genteel citizens picked their careful way over the bodies, pretending they did not exist. How the aliens had confused the social order! What strange alliances had sprouted in the soil turned up by the invasion: Tutu and Terre'blanche, the dynamite twins, united against the common enemy; two nationalisms combined against foreigners in the Beautiful Land. As a black South African, it was almost worth suffering the invasion to experience the fall of the privileged. Except, of course, the aliens were not interested in colour or social class.

Wagenaar stirred and mumbled in his sleep. 'Rika,' he said over and over to himself. 'Rika. *Ek kom.*'

A luminous blue shape seemed to hover there, in the night, where Wagenaar lay. He reached for it, his hands stretching as if he were praying, as if he were asking that thing to enter him. 'Rika,' he said. '*Kom*.'

'Hey, wait, brother!' Patrick Mtetu called. Something had infiltrated their camp, had waited for the right moment (just before death?) to strike. 'Hey, don't talk to that thing!'

'Rika,' the dying man intoned.

'Fucking Martians,' Mtetu swore. He threw himself at the light, but stopped dead in his tracks before he touched it. Fear jammed his lungs so that he could not breathe; it paralysed his legs and froze his hands as if they had been immersed in ice. It forced him to his knees, into the same position as Wagenaar. The fear came from the light.

Wagenaar screamed.

Patrick Mtetu looked up. The blue light was gone; Wagenaar's face was set as hard as stone.

Patrick crawled over to him. 'Hey, are you all right? Don't die on me, man. We must get back to the farmhouse. We'll make it when it gets light. You hear me?'

But Wagenaar was beyond hearing.

'They're waiting for us,' Patrick begged. 'Leon, Levin. Come on, man, they're relying on us.' He shook the Afrikaner by the arms. 'Don't you remember what we went to do?' he shouted into Wagenaar's still face. 'Don't you remember? We went to get information, man. Hey, wake up!' He slapped the stiff cheeks. 'You can't die, man. Brother Tutu sent us to find out where they are. Don't you remember? So we can plan a counter-attack: you know,' his bent arms described a pincer movement, 'like this and like this. Get our own back for Rika and Patience. Hey, fuck you, man, wake up!'

But the chunky farmer flopped in his embrace like Patience had done when they shot her.

'Not you also, brother,' Patrick Mtetu moaned in a soft voice that was on the point of breaking. 'When will this killing stop?'

He held Wagenaar tightly and rocked backward and forward as he hugged him. He wailed, not caring if the aliens heard him, not caring if the mysterious blue light, the death light, reappeared. 'Tutu!' he cried, 'if you speak to God, make Him rid this country of the Martians.'

He buried his face in Wagenaar's neck. The skin felt like wax.

'I'll go and look after your farm for you, brother. I'll plant your fruit trees. I'll sow and I'll harvest. I'll make this place work again. Do you hear me? I'll make your herds grow: sheep, cows, you name it…' His voice died away as he embraced the body.

Everything was absolutely still. The fire was out; the insects and the night birds, the frogs and leopards seemed to have left and gone somewhere else safer, where men did not die on meeting their dead wives. The night eked out its mysteries, lasting forever, until the morning rescued Patrick Mtetu from its spell.

3. Coming in

The old farmhouse had been deserted when the men moved in; its whitewashed walls were as barren as the bareness inside. The new occupants could not make it into a home, nor did they try: in the flight from the cities, not much had been salvaged. Each man took his own room and furnished it as well as he could: a blanket, a foam mattress, a sleeping bag; the luggage of transients. Each man had lost a wife to the aliens: the reason perhaps that each was prepared to risk death himself; perhaps the possibility of death was unimportant, or even welcome. Certainly the occupants of the 'advance lookout post' lived with the knowledge that the aliens could annihilate them at will. Neither the old building nor the ineffectual perimeter wall could offer any resistance to the awesome technology that had brought the country (and possibly the whole world) to its knees. The rusty corrugated-iron roof hardly protected the advance guard from the weather, let alone from the feared alien attack. Living conditions were rudimentary: nothing electrical nor magnetic had worked since the night of the flashing stars. Communications and supplies were carried between the farmhouse and Grahamstown by messengers on horseback. It all seemed hopeless, but it was something to do.

Wagenaar and Mtetu had gone out on their ill-fated mission on orders from the military government in Grahamstown, T'n'T, the Tutu-Terre'blanche alliance. Their brief: to establish where the nearest enemy base was, without making contact.

When they came back, a tall black man wearing dungarees led their horses through the gateway in the stone wall into the front yard. Wagenaar's body was lashed to his horse. Mtetu sat unsteadily in his saddle.

'What happened, Brother Patrick?' the tall man demanded.

'They ambushed us and shot him,' Mtetu wheezed. 'He died in the night. Then they got me. I'm dying, Brother Leon…'

'Hey, Levin!' Leon shouted. 'Come here!'

'They're up to something,' Patrick said. 'Dead wives…'

A small man with a bushy black beard and bald head ran, knobbly-kneed, from inside the house. His watery blue eyes, blinded for a moment in the hard morning light, focused and assessed the scene. 'I told you not to go,' he complained. 'I told you it was madness. But you wouldn't listen to me. Your stupid pride…'

'Shut up and help me,' Leon snapped.

They lay the casualties on the ground, side by side, like any victims from any war.

'Where's Harry?' Mtetu mumbled.

'He's gone back to Grahamstown,' Levin said with contempt. 'You went out for nothing.' He turned away to hide his expression. 'He sent you out and he couldn't even wait.'

'He got scared, man,' grumbled Leon, pulling at one of his gold earrings. 'Fucking politicians.'

'Fucking Martians,' responded Levin. He squatted next to Patrick, staring into the injured man's eyes. He put his hand on Mtetu's forehead; the skin felt clammy.

Something was tugging inside Mtetu's head; through his fuzzy thoughts it tried to get in. Something very important…a face, no body, only the face, with bloodless lips and the calling; the calling that

Wagenaar must have heard. 'Patience,' he said when he recognised her. He stretched out his arm. 'I've missed you.'

'Patience is dead,' said Leon gently. 'They shot her and she died. Don't you remember?'

'Leave him alone.' Levin stood up. He was helpless. Patrick Mtetu was going to die right there in front of him and he could do nothing. 'If he wants to believe that she's here, so what?'

Patrick suddenly saw clearly as if someone had switched channels inside his mind. 'Why did Harry go?' he asked. 'Harry sent us to spy on the Martians, and he didn't wait. Why did Harry go?' The weakness came in waves; Patrick imagined water flowing up a beach and then ebbing out to sea.

'Fucking politicians,' Leon said and laughed nervously. He could cope with the fact of death (he had cut his earrings from the corpse of an elderly white woman in an affluent suburb) but not with the dying. 'What do you say, David?'

'I say nothing,' Levin muttered into his beard. 'He wanted to save himself because he saw how vulnerable we are. And it doesn't make any difference what he tells Grahamstown. Who's to know anyway? So it doesn't matter what I say.'

'That's it,' said Leon. ' 'Do this, do that, serve your country, die. Oh sorry, we've got to go now. Don't worry, be happy.' He punched the air. 'We'd better get you inside and bury him.'

'No!' Patrick urged. 'Don't bury him,' Patience was saying through his lips.

'What?' Leon asked incredulously. 'What d'you mean? Of course we must bury him. He's dead. We can't leave him to rot.' He bent low over Mtetu, preparing to lift him. 'Come, Levin. Help me. He's lying on stones.'

'We're all here together,' said Patience. 'Johan and Rika, and me, and you. And all the others: Rachel…I'll come for you.'

'Don't go!' Patrick screamed and Leon jumped back in fright, scattering clouds of dust into the air like startled chickens.

'What the fuck's wrong with you, man?'

The horses neighed and scratched their hooves in the dirt.

'Patience,' whispered the dying man.

'Is dead. And so is Wagenaar. And I'm very sorry, but we have to bury him. Levin, go and fetch a spade!'

'The mission is not going according to plan,' Patience said. 'The messenger to their leaders fled before we could corrupt him. But we will continue the operation into Grahamstown. I am coming for you now.'

Patrick Mtetu smiled as he died. 'Patience,' he rattled as his head rolled to one side.

'Hey, man, look at that light,' said Leon in wonder.

'It's a fucking ghost,' Levin spat. 'It's his wife!' He ran towards the light.

Whereas Patrick had been struck down by fear, Levin passed right through. Perhaps there had been a slip in the aliens' defence system, perhaps it did not matter that Levin acquired knowledge; he could not use it.

Suddenly he shouted,: 'We must get rid of these bodies!' He began tugging at Wagenaar's shoulders. 'For Christ's sake, help me!' He had become hysterical; he was almost frothing in his anxiety, his beard was speckled with spit. His knees, as thin as the tops of knobkerries, worked in frantic cohesion with his wiry arms. He pulled Wagenaar's body inch by inch along the dirt while he babbled: 'Help me, help me.'

Leon shook his head. '*Die man is mal,*' he said, tapping a finger on his forehead. 'That blue light has scrambled his bookkeeper's brains.' Nevertheless, he got to his knees in the dust. 'You take his arms,' he told Levin, 'and I'll take his legs.'

They carried first Wagenaar and then Mtetu into the barn, laying the bodies on some sacking in the cool darkness. Levin closed the wooden door and jammed a large rock in place as a doorstop. Then, breathless and sweating, he flopped down, resting his back against the barn wall. His legs stuck out of his short grey pants, like grasshoppers'. Leon sat next to him, barefoot, tugging at his earrings. For a long time, neither man spoke.

'Why?' Leon asked eventually. 'What's going on?'

'The aliens are getting in,' Levin said. 'That's what.'

'The bloody aliens can blast us to pieces whenever they want. You know that. Like they did with Cape Town and Port Elizabeth. They could land their machines in this yard and blow us all away.'

'They've got their own way of doing things and I don't understand them either, but that means nothing. I mean, how often did you understand the government?'

Leon nodded in thought, and Levin continued, 'When I went through that light, I knew it belonged to the Martians and that it was taking over Patrick's body.'

'Bullshit,' Leon snorted. 'Listen, man. I'm just a poor stupid township boy like Patrick was. And you're a smart rich whitey. But now there's no more township. And there's no more bookkeepers. So we're all equal now. So don't give me your shit, man.'

'What do you think? Would you rather believe it was a ghost? Patrick's ancestors coming to get him?'

'Maybe. He was talking to his wife. He said something about dead wives…'

'What if they knew that Harry was here? What if they knew he was going back to Grahamstown? What if they planned to take over his body so they could infiltrate the alliance? What if their plans were upset because Harry's already gone, and now they want to take over our bodies? If that makes me a smart whitey, that's fine by me. But that's what I think is going on.'

'I don't accept that theory, Levin,' said Leon quietly. 'They can take over Harry's body just as easily in Grahamstown. They don't give a shit about the alliance. Come, we'd better start digging those graves.'

'So what do they want?'

'Maybe they just want to recruit people to work for them…in the same way the old government used to coopt blacks to their town councils.'

The sun looked down gently through the branches of the dead tree that stood before the front door. It shone on the figures of the grave diggers, bent to their labours.

*

'Rachel,' said Levin and reached for the face that hung tantalisingly close; he felt strangely at peace, he had not been at peace for so long. 'Are you in touch with God?' he asked. 'Or are you a beautiful trap set for us by the enemy?'

'Come to me, David,' said the face with its pale cheeks and dark brown hair, falling in ringlets. The bloodless lips that he used to kiss called him: 'David…David.'

'How d'you know my name?' he asked. 'What do you want with me? You're dead, they shot you, I saw. What d'you want from me?'

The hair would have fallen to shoulders if there had been shoulders. If there had been legs, they would have been long: she had been taller than her husband. If there had been a body, it would have been very thin. David Levin longed for those features: they had attracted him in the beginning; they had been taken away. The need for them constricted his chest. He knew he was dying, he knew the aliens had got him, somehow, perhaps through the blue light, perhaps even when he buried the bodies. In which case, Leon was also having hallucinations. It was too late to warn Leon; it was too late to warn Grahamstown. Not that these warnings would have made the slightest difference: the process was inevitable. The beauty of Rachel's presence lulled and soothed him. It was difficult to move. Weakness settled on David Levin like dust.

4. In Service

Four horsemen rode out of the compound created by the low stone wall. Where their eyes used to be, blue light shone out as if their heads were lanterns containing candles. The men seemed to understand one another without speaking; the eerie silence that reigned over the hills of the Eastern Cape in the early morning was disturbed only by the clip-clopping of hooves. Steam rose from the nostrils of the horses, but not of the men. As one, without seeming to communicate, they turned in the direction of Grahamstown and urged their horses to a gallop.

44

Water Money

The lobster crouched on its bed of rice, legs splayed helplessly. But as the pink seafood dressing seeped into its joints, the creature began to lift its heavy body, painstakingly, from the plate.

'Sit, you bastard!' Attie Labuscagne snarled, waving his knife and fork in tight circles in the air.

Defiantly, the lobster stuck out the stalks of its eyes and with a supreme effort heaved its prehistoric frame, creaking metallically, from the garish mush of rice and sauce.

The diner grunted in annoyance and threw his cutlery down on to the clattering table. He grabbed one thin leg, had it off with a vicious tug, and jammed the limb into his mouth. As he sucked the meat from its cylinder of shell, the lobster squealed in agony.

*

Boetie Mulder flinched awake, gripping the sheet with his fat fingers. He felt the lobster's pain and the full force of Attie Labuscagne's aggression, two refugees from nightmare joined into a single searing image.

Wilma stirred beside him. 'What's wrong?' she mumbled, burying her head in the pillow. 'Go to sleep.'

Outside, the wind gusted and ebbed, rattling the windows.

'I dreamed…' Boetie searched the dark room for the answer, but the image was beyond words. All that came out was, 'I hope the shop's all right.'

'*Ag*, go to sleep,' his wife moaned, rolling over with too much of the sheet.

But Mulder did not reclaim his share. Attie's scowl pushed him up in bed, squirming like a schoolboy before an irate teacher. His back rested against the headboard, his hands clasped on a stomach that ballooned like a pregnant woman's. He reached over to touch Wilma's thin shoulder and the skin felt clammy.

'It's OK. You sleep nicely, hey,' he assured her. 'I'm here. Boetie's here.'

But when he closed his eyes again, the lobster was back, sauce dripping from its knobbled hide like blood. Deforested of legs, it lay on its stomach, just a trunk, while shards of shell mounted on Attie Labuscagne's side plate.

Wilma cuddled up to him in the morning, hopefully stroking his thigh muscles, vestiges of his days on a rugby field. But even if he'd wanted to, Boetie could not dredge up any passion. He kissed her apologetically on the forehead and dressed in his safari suit for work.

*

The manager was wrestling with the maze of figures that head office in Johannesburg had sent down, but he was all at sea. The ring of the telephone stung him out of his bewilderment.

'Hello,' he said sharply.

'Boetie!' the voice was harsh.

'Hello, Attie.' After his dream, speaking to the man was like picking at an open sore.

'Did you get the report?'

'I'm reading it,' Mulder said testily. 'I'm busy reading it.'

'Well, I hope your turnover matches those bloody figures. It's Christmas soon.'

'But Attie, man, the blacks are boycotting white shops here.' He hated the pleading in his voice. 'And our drivers are too scared to deliver in the location because the blacks burn the vans. That's why the turnover's dropping. This is only a small town. It's different in Jo'burg...'

He glanced across the showroom. Lance was sitting at his desk, a welcoming distance from the door, reading the newspaper; Frieda was speaking on the other phone. Neither had heard their boss grovelling, he hoped.

'Listen, my man,' Labuscagne's tone was edged with steel, 'just do your best, hey? Just do your best.'

'By the way,' Boetie ventured, 'I got the water money. I'm going to pay it tomorrow.'

'Good,' Attie seemed to sneer. 'Go ahead.'

He thinks I can't even get that right, Mulder brooded. If I'm so stupid, why did they make me manager? When he put the receiver down, his arm muscle was sore from tension. He pulled a pack of Camels from his top pocket and tapped one out. 'Fuck them,' he said, lighting it.

Lance was leering at him with yellow eyes, and Boetie sucked on his cigarette, returning the stare. But Lance did not meet the challenge. Running his fingers slowly through his thinning hair, he dropped his head and went back to studying the horse racing page. It was ten o'clock and the shop was empty.

An advertising pamphlet mocked Boetie with its sickly pink exuberance and the jingle chimed in his head: 'Your two-year guarantee store.' But no one was making use of the guarantee. The blacks were boycotting because they were always protesting about something or other and the whites either could not afford to buy anything or shopped at the classy House of Oak up the road.

Boetie unlocked his desk drawer nervously, and fingered the white envelope. R239.50. Not enough to steal and risk your job for, but not nice to lose. Mofsowitz, the landlord, would come in tomorrow: he always collected the water money on the twenty-fifth.

Lance sidled over and his boss made a show of shuffling the papers from Jo'burg while closing the drawer with his knee. 'Quiet, hey?'

'*Ja*. What can we do?'

Lance moved the R899 sign from a white couch and sat down. 'Did you go on duty last night?' he asked.

'No. Why?'

'Someone should teach those kaffirs a lesson,' he joked, then added seriously, 'You know, Boetie, I really admire you.'

'Why?' his boss asked with suspicion.

But there was no sarcasm in Lance's reply. 'Because you actually go into the location to make it safer for people like me.'

Mulder's face cleared like a rock pool settling after a storm. 'Well, you can also join the police reserves. We're always looking for more people.'

'*Ag*, no. I'm a coward,' Lance snickered. 'I value my own skin too much.'

'*Ja*, well,' Boetie shrugged. 'It's up to you.'

Mabel arrived with a tray then and the conversation was overtaken by the ritual of morning tea.

*

The lobster pulled itself across the kitchen table, laboriously, inch by aching inch, trying to find its way back to the sea.

'Hey, Pa, why can't we let him go?' the boy pleaded. 'He's hurt.'

The fisherman's violent laugh ricocheted around the room, driving Boetie's flinching mother further into the corner she had occupied since her first husband drowned and she had married this man.

'Because this is money, Boetie my boy…money from the water,' and Pa walloped the table with his fist. 'This is water money!' Roaring with the cheap wine inside him, he picked up the struggling creature, trapping its legs with his huge fingers, and wrenched off its tail. The lobster gasped, bilious from pain.

*

The telephone's piercing alarm woke Boetie Mulder from the dingy room of his childhood. He groped, confused, in the darkness and Wilma grumbled, 'Switch it off.'

'H-h-hello.' Her husband's voice was thick with sleep.

'Hey, Boetie,' the words were spoken urgently. 'It's me, Henry! They've broken into your shop.'

'What?' Lobsters shrieked as they were dropped into boiling water.

'You've had a burglary, my mate. You'd better come over.'

'Oh, shit.' Scalded, Mulder jumped out of bed, still holding the phone, and stubbed his toe on the bedside chair. '*Jou moer*!' he swore. 'No, not you, Henry. What did they take?'

'I don't know. They came in through the roof.'

'OK, I'll be there now.'

Boetie switched on the light. 'I hate that bloody shop,' he burst out bitterly.

'It's your job,' Wilma answered tiredly, 'and I'm sick of it, too.'

'Well, you know how to spend my money!' her husband lashed back. But he got no further reaction.

Wilma buried her head under the pillow.

'I'm the manager but head office doesn't trust me with anything,' he complained. 'They don't give me enough petty cash. I've even got to ask them to send me the money to pay our water account…' A shiver went through him then. 'Even the water money.'

*

Mulder gunned his Mazda into town, taking the corner from Krugerstraat on two wheels. Outside the shop stood the yellow police van, bathed in the pink light of the neon sign. Boetie slammed his foot on the brake, bringing the car to a squealing, skidding stop, and barrelled out, leaving the door open.

A few vagrants, too far gone to be scared of the police, were peering through the shop windows, craning, as if over huge obstacles, to see.

'Go on, *voetsek*!' Boetie bellowed.

'*Ja baas*…shame *baas*,' the ragtag bunch sympathised, peeling away.

Henry, waiting inside, undid the latch.

'How did you know?' Boetie demanded.

'I was on patrol. The door was open.'

Led by his colleague, the manager walked unsteadily down the long diagonal centre aisle, between the lounge suites and the dining-room tables. His legs, which had stood up to countless rugby scrums, were in danger of turning to water and dropping him on the pink vinyl floor. Right in the middle of the ceiling was the hole the black bastards had made, and crawled through like cockroaches.

'Must have had a ladder with them,' Henry mused. 'So tell me, my mate, what's missing? They've broken into that case, I see. Cleaned out all the radios?'

'Fuck them,' Boetie heard himself saying. 'It's not bad enough they boycott my shop. Now they steal from me also…'

He reached his desk, and his biggest fear was realised: the top drawer had been forced open and the white envelope was gone. '*Ag*, no, shit!' he wailed. 'Not the water money.'

Behind his back, he heard Henry chuckling.

'You shouldn't have left it locked up. That's the first place they go for…the locked drawers. Or you should have put it in the safe. *Ja.*'

Irritably, the policeman scratched the back of his head. 'Come, Boetie. You must tell me what they took.'

And the manager, trembling, sat down behind his desk. 'Fuck them all,' he said.

*

It had been a hectic morning, what with the builders to fix the roof and the insurance people, and filling in forms, endless forms. Boetie picked up the receiver and dialled head office. Sweat bubbled at his hairline and was beginning to trickle down his face.

'Hello, Attie. Yes, it's me again.' The lobster was on its back and the hand of authority was poised to twist off its tail. 'Mofsowitz came to fetch the water money and I said they stole it. He's coming back after lunch. What must I do?'

'Whose fault is it, my man?' Attie's tone was so silky sweet he could have been advertising Benson & Hedges. 'I sent it to you. It's your problem.'

'The insurance bloke said they'll only pay in three weeks…'

'You're the manager. Sort it out.'

'Yes, sir,' Boetie choked.

Lance grinned as his boss took out his bank book and opened it at the last entry, checking the balance. And when Mulder crossed the road to Volkskas Bank to draw R239.50 from his account, jackal's eyes followed.

The landlord arrived at half past two, fat and grumbling and short of breath. He did not even say thank you when Boetie handed over the small white envelope containing the water money.

*

'What do you mean you don't have any money for our weekend away?' Wilma demanded. 'You promised!'

'Well…' her husband began, shuffling his feet, 'you know how it is.'

'No, I don't!' She thrust her chin at him and jammed her hands on her hips. 'I don't at all. I slave away for you, wash your clothes, make the food, and once, just once, I ask you to take me away for the weekend, and…' her voice caught on a snag that might have been anger or tears, '…and this!'

Boetie could not explain. Her emotion was like a thick bush that would not allow in the light of reason. Besides, a deep shame flushed through his body, disgrace at everything he was, despised by his wife and his boss and even by Lance, who had no responsibilities at all.

He turned abruptly and left her standing, crooked with distress, in the entrance hall. 'I'm on duty,' he muttered. 'I'll see you in the morning.'

'Go on!' she screamed. 'Go and play cops and robbers with your mates! See if I'm here when you get back!'

'You've got nowhere else to go,' he retorted.

*

'Hey, what's wrong?' Louis asked. 'You're quiet tonight.'

'*Ag*, it's nothing.' She blamed him for everything; she was always moaning. And Attie was always picking at his skin. And the bloody kaffirs had stolen the water money.

Louis was driving; the dark township streets yielded flitting figures, cut into small squares by the protective mesh on the police van's windows. The radio was on, but only static crackled through. Someone had put a sticker on the back: LOVE A COP. THEY CARE.

'It gives me the fucking creeps to drive in here,' Louis grumbled, and when Boetie did not answer, he added, with an attempt at cheerfulness, 'I suppose someone's got to stop them from rioting, hey?'

The knives were out, and the lobster was going to get it. Any minute now, stones would spit on the sides of the van, on the roof, would crunch into the mesh. Didn't they throw a hand grenade into Sakkie's lap the other week, and thank Christ it didn't go off or he'd have lost his balls that's for sure. Boetie had his 9mm Parabellum ready, just in case.

'You're an idiot!' Wilma howled. 'You work for peanuts and you can't even take me away for a weekend.'

'What did you say?' Boetie asked aloud.

'Nothing,' Louis replied, concentrating on the road. 'Why?'

But the question was left hanging like the mist of cold breath in the air between them. Transfixed in the headlights in the middle of the road was a young black boy. Louis jerked the wheel viciously.

'Fuck it…!' Boetie cocked the pistol, aimed roughly at the figure that slid past his window, and pulled the trigger. His wrist jerked with the gun's recoil. When it levelled, he fired again, and again. The explosions packed the cabin with noise and the acrid smell of cordite.

'What are you doing?' Louis yelled as the boy went down and the police van choked to a stop.

'It's war,' Boetie grated. 'It's them or us.'

Pistols cocked, eyes beginning to burn, the policemen sat, waiting for a move from the darkness. But, apart from a ringing in the ears, everything was deadly still; nothing stirred.

'Better take a look,' Mulder said at last, hefting his weight into the street.

His shoes grated on small stones as his torch punched a hole in the night, unveiling the dead boy's face. Two white moons, fixed on something Boetie could not see, threw back the light. A bullet had hit the boy in the chest, punching through his school jersey, and a wet, black pool soaked the ground beneath him. A trickle of blood had leaked from a corner of his mouth and was running down his chin. He could not have been more than twelve.

'Come and help me,' Mulder said.

Louis's door clicked open, a lonely sound. '*Ag*, no, Boetie,' he said sourly when he saw the body. 'You didn't have to shoot him.'

From behind the windows of the council houses, lit by candles because there was no electricity in the location, eyes followed them and curtains fluttered closed. But the movement could have been caused by the wind from the sea, or perhaps the thin moon, skulking behind shifting cloud, deceived. The police van's twin white headlights bored into the township, but illuminated nothing, ultimately dying in the gravel.

'You take his legs. I'll take his arms.'

The boy was as heavy and limp as a slaughtered sheep; he left a trail of blood and meat on the ground as the two policemen grunted and groaned him on to the cold metal floor of the van. Boetie picked up a few rocks and tossed them in as well, not caring about the noise. No grieving mother came wailing out at them as they climbed wearily back into the cabin. No angry mob sought a rough township justice.

'He was an agitator,' Boetie insisted to break the silence that had iced over between them. 'Just say he was throwing rocks at us. There, I've brought the rocks as evidence. It'll be all right.'

'It's not all right,' Louis protested. 'After those kaffirs broke into your shop, it looks bad. It looks like revenge.'

'*Ag*, man, don't worry. We'll make our report. Nobody saw us. And even if they were looking from those houses, it was too far away and it was dark. No one will believe them. Just back me up, OK?'

'*Ja…ja*, sure.'

'Well then, shake on it.'

As their hands met, a wild gush of laughter erupted in the blind cabin. 'Hey, it's funny, Boet,' Louis wheezed. 'You sell them furniture in the day and then you shoot them at night.'

'*Ja*, that's how it is ,' Mulder replied somberly.

Racked by laughter, Louis managed to start the engine and the van wobbled out of the township, its obscene cargo sliding and bumping at every turn.

'We'll have to get Moses to wash out the blood at the station,' Boetie said, then added, 'I need a drink. Drive to my house.'

'OK.'

*

The police van slowed as it approached the turn-off to the white suburbs. On the corner, a blue gum tree fractured the orange light from a street lamp. The rays drove luminous wedges into the mist.

'Looks like a picture in a Bible, hey?' Louis said quietly, his mirth exhausted.

'*Ja*. I s'pose so.'

The van slid easily through the tidy streets, past cars without souls, stopping at last beside a garden wall punctuated by four ox-wagon wheels. Louis reversed to the front gate. Inside the small house, a bedroom light was on, dimly, as if the occupant were reading before she fell asleep.

'I won't be a minute.' Boetie sniffed noisily. 'Just wait for me.'

'Well, hurry up,' Louis said. He flicked his head towards the back. 'I don't like to sit here alone with that.'

There was no car in the street to warn him.

The policeman scraped his key in the lock and pushed open the front door. Did he hear scurrying, as if mice were at work in the bedroom? He called out, 'Wilma…!'

'No, Boet,' she managed in a strangled voice.

Her husband's bulk filled the entire space of the doorway. She could not hide the thin strands of hair that belonged to someone else in the bed. A pair of frightened eyes peered out from under the sheets.

Boetie's holster was already unclipped. He wrenched out the pistol and, with a sleight of hand, cocked it. A dull click announced that a bullet had entered the chamber.

'Lance!' He hawked the name out of his throat.

The shop assistant said nothing, but his pale yellow eyes stared into the hole of the barrel, mesmerised like a meercat in a car's headlights. Mulder's finger whitened on the trigger as he focused the pistol on a point just below the man's hairline. He saw again the gaping wound in the black boy's chest where his previous bullet had entered. What difference would a second death make?

But Pa's drunken voice was roaring through Boetie's madness. 'You bitch!' the fisherman screamed as he laid his boot into the bleeding woman on the floor. 'I'm on the boats from morning to night and you spend my money on school books!'

'No, Pa!' the boy squealed. 'Leave my mother alone!'

A vicious blow sent Boetie reeling across the kitchen table into the mess of lobster shells that were the remains of Sunday lunch.

Mulder shook his head to repel the memories of that raw wind-swept past. An incessant sobbing was hammering for his attention, demanding to be let in; it came from Wilma. He allowed his arm to drop. They looked so pathetic snivelling in bed together.

Savagely, Boetie pulled open a drawer and rummaged among his underwear for the bottle of brandy he kept hidden there. Clutching it by the neck like a strangled gull, he dragged his feet out of the house leaving the front door open.

At the gate, shoulders drooping, he hesitated, weighing up whether to go back or to go on. For a moment he stood perfectly still, balanced, brandy in one hand and gun in the other. Then he teetered forward, and Louis started the engine.

Fountains

'In my dream, my mother's father came to me,' Sam said, 'and sent me to Ma Bongwe. I mean, what chance did we have with stones against Hippos?'

I nodded, and leaned forward. The single candle flickered as a cold wind from the sea insinuated its way through cracks where the corrugated iron sheets overlapped. I sat on a corner of the bed; Sam hunched on the floor.

'Write these things down,' he insisted. His finger jabbed, stiff as a *kierie*.

'I don't take notes,' I told him, tapping my forehead. 'I remember. It's safer.'

'All right,' he conceded, 'just don't miss anything. Just get it right.'

The candle sent shivers of light through the shack, but Sam's face was hidden under a balaclava. Only his eyes and his lips were free.

'Do you know about our ancestors?' he asked and, before I could answer, he said, 'They look after us.' His voice quivered, betraying his growing excitement. 'They help us in the struggle. The Boere have the guns, but we have the ancestors. They speak to us in our dreams.'

The previous night I had also dreamed: of a bomb exploding in a crowded restaurant. Chairs took off like pelicans surprised by thunder, and flapped clumsily through the glass shopfront. Diners, dumped in the mess of their meals, wondered if they were still in this world or already in the next. But neither fire nor shrapnel assaulted my eyes. Instead, a fountain of water flowered from the epicentre of the blast and crashed heavy drops on my head. I woke sodden with sweat.

'In the UDF we used to organise mass meetings,' Sam was saying.

'We had a lot of support in the townships. But,' he added bitterly, 'that was before the UDF was banned like the ANC. We wanted peaceful change. But the government keeps pushing us into a corner. And you know what happens then.'

An engine gunned outside and Sam started up anxiously. But the noise receded and his shoulders slumped once more.

'The funeral was on a Sunday,' he began. Pensively, he stuck his thumb into his mouth and gnawed at the nail.

The smell of meat and onions, cooked on a paraffin stove, lingered mustily in the shack. Out in the night, a dog yelped and another answered.

'Whose funeral?' I prompted.

'A comrade,' Sam replied. 'The police shot him the week before, also at a funeral. That's how it went in those days. One funeral led to the next.'

He tugged at the balaclava as if it were suffocating him. 'We needed protection and Ma Bongwe was a *sangoma*, a witchdoctor,' he explained in case I didn't understand, but I did. 'Three of us, the leaders, went to see her on Sunday morning after my dream.'

He cleared his throat and I thought – not for the first time – how young the 'leadership' often was: with their elders in jail or in exile or dead, teenagers were at the forefront of the struggle.

I did not hurry him; he was very nervous and I could wait all night if necessary. After all, *he* had called *me* to arrange the interview.

'She was old and thin like my grandmother and dressed all in white with necklaces and bangles of bones and shells,' Sam said at last. 'Man, it was quite scary when she shivered and moaned and rattled because we knew she was in touch with the ancestors. They'd warned her we were coming and she'd got her special *muti* ready for us…'

An icy draught grabbed hold of my neck then and I hugged myself for warmth. Sam did not seems to notice the cold, although how his thin tracksuit could protect him was a mystery to me.

'Ma Bongwe told us that the ancestors backed our mission,' he was saying. 'They didn't want any more of our people to die. And then she lit some incense and soon the house was full of thick smoke. She said it was to keep the Boere away.'

'And,' I prodded when Sam fell silent, 'did it?'

'Of course, man,' he snapped. 'The ancestors were on our side. No cop could have got into that house with its smoke.'

He rubbed his palms vigorously up and down his thighs as if generating the energy to continue. 'But, shit, Ma Bongwe was making a lot of noise,' he chuckled. 'She was rattling her beads and stamping her feet and groaning like she was sick. When she stopped, it was very quiet. Then she took a pouch from inside her skirt and gave it to me. And she said, "Take this powder and hold some in your hands. You must blow it into the air and call, 'Botha…Le Grange…you have no power over us…Botha…Le Grange…you have no power.' You'll see what will happen." That was Ma Bongwe's magic.'

'What was this powder?' I asked when Sam hesitated again.

'She said it would make the soldiers go to sleep,' he answered slowly as if he had just been woken. 'She said, "Then be quick! Pick up their guns and shoot them."

'But we were frightened. "Mama! We aren't murderers!" we cried.

'But she just said, "I'm telling you what the ancestors want."

'Then she took a stick like a fork and she put it into her bucket of *muti*. She rubbed it between her hands – you know, like a Bushman lighting a fire – and the foam began to rise up, up, until it reached the top.

'She said, "If this foam falls over, I'll know the plan is going well. Otherwise the plan has not worked."

'"What then, Mama?" we asked. "What if something goes wrong?"

'But she jumped up, shouting, "Go now!" And then she started singing again, and I was so sure my grandfather was there that I was afraid. The three of us ran out of her house and it was only on the corner that I remembered I was still holding the pouch.'

So engrossed was I in Sam's story that I jerked in alarm when a lion coughed in the road opposite the shack. Sam had grown rigid as though his spirit had flown, leaving only the husk of his body behind. But the Casspir rumbled away and gradually Sam's fingers unclenched.

'I can't talk too long,' he muttered. 'I've been here too long already.'

'Finish your story,' I urged, fearing he would leap out into the night as suddenly as he had dashed in, a rabbit from the dunes.

'Of course,' he retorted. 'Well, the funeral took place and we were marching up the road towards the cemetery. In front, a group of comrades held the coffin on their shoulders and, behind, the people were full up like sardines. And there I was, toyi-toying and blowing this powder from my hands, and singing, like Ma Bongwe said, "Botha…Le Grange…you have no power!"'

Sam exhaled sharply, his breath breaking the candlelight into a hundred shards. 'And over there the Hippos were waiting, three of them, where they'd stood the week before – where they waited every week – on that patch of open ground on the way to the cemetery.' He licked the corners of his mouth and studied his chewed nails.

'What happened?' I asked urgently.

The young man straightened his back and clenched his fist. 'As Ma Bongwe had said, every single one of those soldiers was asleep. It was what the ancestors wanted. And I saw it with my own eyes. Even those on the ground just lay next to their guns, fast asleep, stretched out.' He shook his head. 'Man, it was wonderful.'

A gust of wind rattled the loose sheets of corrugated iron and a strong smell of seaweed invaded the shack. Shadows and light catapulted into the rows of tomato soup labels that papered the walls.

'And did you take their guns?' I asked.

'Oh no!' he protested. 'The UDF was not violent. We couldn't do that. But you must understand, there were so many people, and we were so excited…even trying to keep the crowd quiet was noisy. And so, naturally, the soldiers woke up…' He pulled absently at the thread in the carpet which was the shack's only floor.

'I was standing there with this powder in my hands,' he said, 'and the soldier closest to me picked up his rifle. He didn't know why he was lying on the ground – he had to wipe the sleep from his eyes. He pointed the gun at me…and I suppose that Ma Bonwe's foam fell inside the bucket. Because a miracle happened! When he pulled the trigger and I thought I was going to die because I'd disobeyed my ancestors, nothing came out of the barrel but a fountain of water!'

'I don't believe it!' I exclaimed.

'They were so surprised! Every time they pulled their triggers, only water sprayed out of their guns.' He laughed, despite his nervousness. 'They were like children with water pistols. They were so terrified when we pushed closer to them, shouting, "*Amandla!*" and waving our fists. They believed their last day had dawned. But we didn't touch a hair on their heads. We just danced past them to the cemetery… It was the funeral that broke the chain,' he added. 'No one was injured, and there was no funeral the next Sunday.'

'How can I write a story like that in the newspaper?' I demanded. 'My editor will laugh at me.'

He shrugged. 'It doesn't matter if you do or you don't. I'm telling you. I was there.' He punched his fist into the palm of his open hand. 'They banned the UDF,' he said angrily. 'They closed down the voice of peace and reason. And I decided to follow the other route…I had no choice. You must warn the whites of the consequences if they stifle the voices of peace.'

He stood up tiredly – he was a small stocky man – and extended his hand. We shook, the threefold clasp popular in the townships.

'Maybe the ancestors have punished us after all,' he reflected, opening the door of the shack. 'Well, goodbye my friend. I won't be seeing you again.'

I did not move. I sat, with my notebook open, its blank pages resting on my knees.

'Goodbye,' I replied to the darkness of the shackland, as fountains of bombs exploded in the night.

Dog Training

'I had to shoot him,' Eddie said, locking his fingers together and squeezing his knuckles until they were white. 'I didn't have a choice. It was him or me.'

'Then you can't blame yourself,' Maria replied.

'It was war,' Eddie explained. 'He was a terrorist. I don't blame anyone.'

Maria stole a glance towards the bedroom as if someone were in there, but he knew she was alone. 'I didn't expect you to come,' she said. 'You should have phoned first.'

'Why?' he bristled. 'I'm not exactly a stranger.' His big hand hugged the beer can she had found in the fridge for him. 'I know I've been away for nearly a year, but I'm not a stranger. Am I?'

'No, of course not, Eddie,' she said but she did not go on and, in the stillness, his mind began to wander as it used to in the bush. He saw again the startled expression on the dead black face before the horror of what he had done drove him puking out into the burning village.

'We met so long ago,' he said and his mouth was dry despite the beer.

'You were still at school,' she replied, using the word like a hammer to nail up the past.

'And you had just left your husband.' He grinned, crookedly, triumphantly. 'You loved me then, didn't you?'

She nodded and reached for a cigarette. The top of her gown fell open and Eddie shivered with desire as he imagined her small breasts beneath the coarse red fabric.

'Didn't you?' he demanded, conscious of a swelling in his crotch.

'Yes, Eddie,' she answered nervously, pulling her gown tighter as if she were drawing a curtain.

'It's not my fault I had to go into the army,' he grumbled and he tipped his head back, pouring the bitter liquid into his mouth. 'For two bloody years,' he gurgled, 'and it's still not over.'

'No, it isn't.' Her face was pinched and there were a few more lines around her eyes. 'But it's been hard,' she said, 'for me and the kids.'

'Why? Hasn't he paid the maintenance?'

'Some months he pays, some months he doesn't. It's just hard being a single parent. I don't like to leave my babies alone all day.'

'Why don't you get a babysitter?'

'A girl comes in…'

'Well, that's OK then.'

'No, it's not,' she snapped. 'I worry. You don't have children. You don't know what it's like leaving them.'

'*Ja*, I can imagine,' he said to mollify her.

'No, you can't,' she retorted.

Squirming at her sudden hostility, he tried to bury himself in the armchair. He stretched out his long legs and surveyed the sparsely furnished room. A sliding door led to a balcony that overlooked the beachfront. On the sideboard stood a photograph of a boy and a girl, taken on the beach: the girl was laughing, the boy squinted into the camera. He had his mother's frown.

'Where are the kids?' Eddie asked, looking around.

'They've gone to my mom for the weekend.'

'Oh?' he raised his eyebrows. 'I'd have thought you'd want to be with them.'

'I was tired,' she said. 'I had a hard week.'

He shook his head miserably, trying to believe her.

She pulled on her cigarette and blew out smoke. 'You're still in uniform,' she commented as if she had only just noticed.

'I came straight over. I wanted to see you.'

She bunched her fists. 'That's nice.'

'We left Pretoria yesterday morning. We drove right through the night.'

'You must be exhausted.'

'I could get into bed,' he hinted, but she did not take up the offer.

They had not touched, except for the brief kiss at the door when he smelled smoke in her hair, and later when she gave him the beer and their fingers grazed.

A helicopter clattered outside and Eddie leaped up; he reached the sliding door in two strides, pulled it open and stepped onto the balcony. Maria followed more slowly and stood next to him.

The beachfront was dressed in yellow for battle: police vans, mobile dog cages, even a Casspir, mingled uneasily with the holiday crowd.

'It's those bloody agitators,' she muttered, screwing up her eyes in the sharp sunlight.

'*Ja*, I know. There was a roadblock on the freeway. The police were stopping all the blacks.'

'They've got their own beaches. Why must they come here and cause trouble?'

He shook his head and put his arm around her. 'We went to the border because that's where the war was. Now when I come back, it's right outside your flat.'

For a moment she leaned against him. 'A bomb went off in a toilet down there last night.' She pointed and he felt a tremor ripple through her thin shoulder.

'Is that why you sent the kids to your mom?'

'*Ja*.' She nodded slowly, evaluating this explanation.

'Well, it's all under control now,' he said.

From the glassy edge of the water up to the road, the white sand was deserted except for policemen and their dogs. Red and white striped tape cordoned off the entire length of the beach and on the shower cubicles were notices: DANGER – POLICE DOG TRAINING.

'It's a bit of a joke,' he said. 'Dogs aren't even allowed on the beach.'

'Who's laughing?' she asked sourly.

She pulled away and his arm dropped uselessly to his side.

On the beach, a line of Alsatians, tails flicking excitedly, faced a line of men. At a hidden signal, the dogs strutted over to their handlers, heads high, lolling tongues pulling back their lips in laughter. The policemen then marched away in step, or pretending to get into step, dogs at their heels.

Maria glanced at her watch as if she was expecting someone to return and Eddie suddenly felt very tired. He noticed the statuette of an African woman, carved out of a dark wood, that lay neglected on the rusty veranda table. The woman's breasts were uncovered. It reminded him of the bush. But the sharp smell of the sea brought him back to the present.

'I've hardly slept for two days,' he said, rubbing his eyes. 'We drove through the night. I wanted to get back to see you.'

She did not answer, but seemed to become smaller. Her mouth was a grim line; the skin of her forehead wrinkled in a frown.

'I was in the bush for months,' he said, 'and it was hard for me also. But thinking about you made it easier. Here, I've got your picture.'

He fumbled in his top pocket and pulled out a wallet. She accepted the photograph with uncertain fingers and studied the younger, smiling woman before handing her back.

'I spoke about you so often,' he said, 'that the other guys used to mock me...'

'Eddie,' she interrupted, sliding her feet in and out of her slippers, but she could not deflect him.

'You kept me going. What else was I in the bush for? For this? Nothing's changed. It's getting worse!'

'Don't shout. The neighbours will hear.'

'I don't care about the neighbours! You didn't write. Didn't you get my letters?'

He leaned over the parapet, almost too far, and her eyes widened with alarm.

'I got them,' she replied in a calm, measured voice.

'And when I phoned from Pretoria, there was no reply. What's going on?' he asked harshly, drawing back from the edge and standing up straight.

She looked directly into his eyes for the first time. 'I'll tell you what, Eddie. Last time you were here…when you left, I was pregnant.'

He was on the point of putting the beer can to his lips but his hand froze, then fell. Inside the flat, a fly buzzed futilely against a window pane, trying to get out.

'But you were taking the pill,' he said weakly.

'I stopped for a while to give my body a rest. It doesn't matter now.'

'So what happened? Why didn't you tell me?'

'What was the point? I lost the baby. I was in hospital for a few days.' Her eyes were green, accusing. 'What would I have done with your baby? You couldn't have supported me and a baby anyway.'

He slammed his fist into the wall and she winced.

'What was the point of telling you? I lost it anyway.' There was a hard line around her eyes.

He turned again to the events below, watching absently, trying to fit together the information she had dropped like a grenade into the space between them. His fist was numb and he wondered if he had broken it.

An elderly black man, a lonely determined figure, strode up to the police cordon. A ragged cheer from the protesters lifted him over the tape and carried him across the ice of the sand without scuffing it, to the water's edge. As he passed the BEACH: WHITES ONLY sign, he spat.

Policemen and their dogs swivelled in anger and people, unshackled, spilled out of restaurants and cafés. Dressed in T-shirts calling for non-racial beaches, waving toy buckets and spades, they flooded the dry white sand.

'How did you lose it?' Eddie asked. 'The baby. What happened?'

Maria was rubbing the bare place on her finger where she used to wear a wedding ring. Her hands jerked when a loudhailer blared, 'This beach has been reserved for dog exercises. You have five minutes to disperse!'

Eddie swallowed the last of the beer and hurled the can at a young white man running with the blacks. 'Fucking Commie!' he yelled. His hand was beginning to hurt as the numbness wore off and he turned on Maria. 'Why didn't you tell me about the baby? I had a right to know!'

'It wouldn't have helped.' Her face settled then as if she had reached a decision and she stood taller than before. 'Eddie, I'm sorry. But you must go now.'

He rubbed his eyes; the rising pain in his hand had gone to his brain. He was not sure if he had heard her correctly. 'But I've only just got here,' he said. 'Where must I go?'

Anxiety raised the pitch of her voice. 'You must go now. Martin is coming any minute.'

'Who?' he said in disbelief. 'Who's coming?' Panic raked his stomach as it had done when he kicked down the door of the hut in that faraway village and he found himself staring into the hollow eye of an AK-47. His fingers sought out and fastened on the statuette of the African woman, and he gripped it like a club.

'Eddie, put that down,' Maria said firmly. 'You don't want trouble.' But her lower lip was trembling and she reached in her pocket for a cigarette.

'Who is he?' Eddie panted. 'Has he been around long?'

'He was very kind to me…after I lost the baby.'

'Is he a doctor?'

'He's got a job. He's older, Eddie. Older than you.'

The helicopter whined past again and Eddie blindly took in the beachfront chaos. The police were wading into the almost-picnicking crowd, quirts flailing, faces smiling with the pleasure of contact. The burly men fell over one another, competing with their dogs to get in first. The protesters scattered as a policeman with a video camera captured their faces for his files and the helicopter squatted on the beach, sending up gales of sand.

Eddie lowered the statuette and leaned against the wall that he had punched. He was white around the mouth and his shoulders slumped. 'When's he coming back?'

'Any minute.'

Plastic buckets and spades and sandwich wrappers and picnic baskets rose into the air in a whirlwind created by dogs and policemen and frantic demonstrators.

Eddie sighed. 'How could you do it, Maria?'

'Just go.' Her eyes were frightened although her voice was firm. Her mouth was obscured by smoke.

But Eddie flexed his wrist, rocking the statuette back and forth, beating its head into the cupped palm of his free hand. 'I sat in the bush for you,' he said simply. 'I don't really care what I do now.'

'Don't be mad!'

'You know what?' Eddie smiled bleakly. 'After I shot that terrorist, I felt so much power. I'd actually killed another man.'

Maria stepped back. 'But Eddie, that was war. You're allowed to in war.'

'I'd been bothered about why he didn't shoot first. He had me in his sights and I still had to bend to get into the hut. I thought maybe he didn't want to wake his kids. You know, sometimes you think nonsense. But when I checked, I found he didn't have any bullets. I shot an unarmed man.'

'You didn't know.'

Tears were streaming down Eddie's cheeks. 'But I loved it,' he cried. 'It was good.'

'Eddie, this isn't war.'

Down below, a series of sharp reports pricked the tranquil morning and a cloud of tear-gas spread like sea mist over the beach. People were sprinting away from the crying fog, dropping jackets and sunglasses as they nursed their wounded eyes, while on a lamp post a National Party election poster pleaded: GIVE F.W. A CHANCE, and the bald party leader beamed down on the disappearing street with his enigmatic smile.

And then the tear gas from the war to keep South Africa white drove Eddie and Maria back into the safety of her flat.

His fingers curled like a wedding band around the naked statue's breasts as the key turned in the lock and the front door began to open.

Martin stood there, a startled, dumb look on his civil servant's face, armed only with a bunch of flowers.

The pain coursed through Eddie's exhausted frame, from his smashed hand to his bloodshot eyes. He saw the AK-47 poking through the door of the hut in the black village and then the power rose up and overwhelmed him.

Gone Fishing

1. Major Tertius du Preez

I find myself aiming along the curve of the rod as I used to peer through the telescopic sight of a rifle. I watch the tip, wait for it to bob, anxious for the adrenalin pump as the prehistoric creature in the depths takes the bait I've so carefully prepared: a meal of death, the last supper – honeyed bread lovingly kneaded into paste.

And, steel through its bony cheek, the fish will plunge away from that taunting, invisible line into the muddy water. I shall let it run, keeping up the tension as it sounds, searching for a rock on which to tangle the snare and cut itself free to spend the rest of its days with my piece of obscene jewellery gouged into its face.

Taut. Hold the rod up. Head the cold, calculating creature away from obstructions. The light tackle highlights my skill. I will play with you, monster from the deep, until, exhausted, you will succumb to my gentle persuasion and will enter my net, and there you will be mine. You will be my prisoner – and I am used to taking prisoners, or I was before I ended up in this backwater.

My huge, calloused hands exhort magic from the quivering wand. They jerk and reel in and let go and allow my prey to run for a few exhilarating moments before flicking again. They have a mind of their own; they know what to do without any instruction from my brain, those hooked machines. Perfect harmony – flesh and gut and fibreglass – working as a team to achieve the objective; that is how it should be and I am filled with contentment.

But there is another, perhaps even greater, pleasure in being here: I am at the peaceful heart of the storm. On either bank of the river a wall of dark green trees keeps evil at bay while the sun illuminates the centre, raising chuckles on the crests of the small grey waves. A light wind picks up, brushing the intoxicating smell of the river against my nostrils, lapping the gentle water against my rubber boots. Only occasionally do I think I hear a rustle and I glance over my shoulder, trying to decipher the shadows among the tree trunks, but it is nothing, not even a spider dangling from a line cast by the branches. No, the sound has an altogether more sinister origin than that: it is a whisper from the grave. For a moment, the sun blinks and goes out, but that is only a cloud come to spoil the warm moments of my retirement.

We played them like fishes, and their dead eyes and gaping mouths resembled not much more nor less than those of the carp or bass I pull in to die horribly on the grass.

The shiver from the shadows in the forest has leapt and rushed along the fuse which has its end point in this simple fisherman. I reel in. There were no explosions of fury today, no boiling water from a crazed fighter hooked and ready to confront me with everything it's got.

I jam my khaki hat down over my thinning hair, catch sight of my stomach swaggering beyond the confines of my trousers: I am the caricature of an Afrikaner; all I need is a beer can and cheeks full of broken veins and then a cartoonist can make a *boerewors* meal of me. How I have lost condition during my retirement!

As I pack up, I rejoice in the visual richness: mountains peak over the serried ranks of dark pine trees, layer above layer, colours that resonate deeply in the soul of this comical Afrikaner: my country.

My country, I say! And, at my feet, the mottled river concealing who knows what in its subconscious depths. White water as the breeze freshens and the rapids punish the black rocks… I have retired to a beautiful part of my land.

They made a mistake with me. They didn't realise how valuable I was to them: all my knowledge, my experience, my contacts – and they put me out to pasture. Thank you very much, you did a good job while we needed that kind of thing, but now times have changed and you are a liability to us, no longer an asset on the balance sheet of state necessities. In fact, you've become a bit of an embarrassment, so here's your envelope and please go and bury yourself out of the way before we bury you ourselves, so we can bury the hatchet with our former foes instead of in their backs. *Ja.*

All I can add is that thank God my dear Bessie did not live to see this day – what they've done to me, how they've stripped me of my uniform and my power. Poor Bessie. She was so proud of her husband, the soldier. Sometimes at night I can still hear her singing *Die Stem* at the medal ceremonies, her voice rising like those mountain peaks above the mediocrity of the others, her small fists clenched in passion, in belief at what we were doing.

I just followed policy. OK, I made some of my own decisions, but that's what I was there for; that's why I was so good, why they promoted me. I was a scholar of war.

War, and the evolution of a nation, are like that: yesterday's enemy is today's ally, which turns me into the enemy. Ironic isn't it? I have studied these things. And all the while, in the depths of that watery mind, below the surface of the river, the sleek silver bodies torment me with their knowledge of affairs that I still had to find out. And my silver hook, trawling in the caverns of that labyrinthine intelligence, seeks the answer.

But I still keep my hand in. This appearance of retirement is misleading. I will not let my talents go to waste. I will continue to serve my country. Not this new country that my former employers are trying to create, in league with our enemies, but the country my forefathers conquered with their blood. The country in which my Bessie is laid to rest. On her sick bed, just before she died, Bessie said that the days of the Republic are over, that now the blacks will spit into Blood River and they will light fires on the floor of the Voortrekker Monument. I swore to her I would not let these things happen.

These murky depths in the river are nothing compared to the murky business I have become involved in. I still recognise the face of my enemy. I will not let them steal my land. I may be packing up for the day, but I will be back: my fishing is by no means over.

2. Vuyo Mpaka

The cars have kept me awake. Every time I start to fall asleep, there is a whoosh, and I am up again. Each car is another number in the countdown to when I rise for my greatest moment.

The coldest time is just before the dawn breaks over those hills and the sweat has dried on my body and stiffened my clothes, but I don't mind the discomfort. In fact, I rejoice in the hardship. When I stand up, I have to kick to unloosen my locked joints; I blow out like a great steam engine: choo-choo-choo. But I am going nowhere. Just standing and watching and waiting and smacking my lips at the expectation of the moment to come. The ghost of my breath punctuates the chilly air with exclamation marks. The cars are whooshing past, but the time has not yet arrived. I will know when all the pieces are in the right place.

The calabash moon is being swallowed by clouds – it will be dark before it is light – and I am as calm as that moon. But then anger grabs my stomach like a fist over a hand grenade and blind fury makes its own light in the pre-dawn sky, and the dust in my joints turns to burning oil.

Who knows where they came from? Perhaps from the hostel on the hill – that great evil castle on the skyline where the migrant workers live. Outcasts from afar, never accepted by the residents, they are open to be bribed by the highest bidder; criminal gangs hide out there, agents of the government, or whatever sinister groups have now taken over from the government in trying to keep apartheid alive.

My mother had not switched off the lights because we were still busy in the house before we went to sleep. The pot of water for our last cup of tea was still boiling on the primus stove. My little brother – he was in standard 6 – heard the shouting before I did and stood up from his homework. He opened the curtains to look out and I remember scrambling to get a chair out of the way so I could pull him down, before…

Who knows where they came from? A white car drives into our township, swollen with assassins, long guns lean out of windows and blast away whoever is unlucky enough to be in the way: a husband stumbling outside sleepily to pee, a young man off to work in the early morning, partygoers returning too late, lovers necking under a bus shelter. Random killing because they want to spread fear and to derail negotiations for a democratic future; they are the whites' 'third force' and they do not care who their victims are.

Mrs Vilikazi from next door was screaming but I could not make out her words. My brother dropped his books: I saw his mouth fall open but the chair was in the way and I could not reach him in time. My mother flicked off the lights and, in the sudden darkness, I saw flashes from the street. Someone was yelling, 'Get down! Get down!' and I think it was me. Then the bullets ripped through the windows and I thought they would never stop. There was a terrible explosion but, in trying to get to my brother, I'd knocked over the table and it shielded me from the blast. All I knew was that I had to help my mother and the boy. But the flames were out of control. They were wild, mad animals, eating whatever their crackling tongues licked on. The heat forced me away from that part of the house where my mother was, where a bullet must have punctured the gas cylinder and sent us to hell. I crawled out of that house of fire while my family was cooked. Lucky for my father that he ran away years ago: maybe he died somewhere else.

Who were these people? Why was it so important for them to kill my brother and my mother, a woman who had never harmed anyone in her life? What could they gain from destroying my house?

People say that it was the white soldiers or police who don't want the blacks to gain majority rule, that they are trying to destabilise the country before we can have an election. Others say it was the Zulus who live in that hostel on the hill because they want their own country.

Or maybe it was both of these groups together. Police helping Inkatha to murder our people. You can hire men for a thousand rand to kill for you. They have no political affiliation – they will do anything to put food in their stomachs.

These guesses, even if one of them is true, will not bring back my mother and my brother. In the morning, their charred bodies were found in the ashes of our house. There was hardly enough to scrape together for a decent funeral. The police arrived, of course, to look for clues, but that's a joke because they investigate nothing: how can they investigate themselves?

I don't know where I spent the night; I cannot remember. Neither can I remember the days after the attack. There were meetings, apparently, and angry speeches at the funerals of all the victims, and the newspaper wrote stories about the massacre, although no one asked me for my story.

Some of those who lost family took revenge on the houses of the black policemen who live in our township; petrol bombs were thrown through windows, even cars were set alight. There was a march to the hostel on the hill, but the police were there in their Hippos, to protect their allies, and they shot at our people with live ammunition. The spiral of violence, they call it: more marches, more deaths, more funerals.

But I was not involved in any of this. I was mad, I went to visit my ancestors to seek some advice. I was a spirit; I wanted to know from the spirits of those who watch over our affairs on Earth from their special place what I could do to allow my mother and brother to rest in peace. I spent a long night with my great-grandfather who had fought against the Boers on the banks of the Fish River. We sat at a campfire and, sometimes, when he was making a point, he stood up and leaned on his spear. He is a very clever old man; his wisdom comes from studying the course of our history for two hundred years, and he told me the answer. Then he gave me a bowl of porridge with special medicine to make me strong, and he sent me back into this world.

I woke in hospital and I discharged myself as soon as I could stand up and find my clothes. The nurses tried to hold me back, but I shook them away and I hitched a lift back to my township. My house was destroyed but Mrs Vilikazi let me stay with her for the time being.

One day, when I was well, I went to the squatter camp and met a man who had been pointed out to me. He had an AK-47, just brought in from Mozambique, and, as I handed him forty rand, I knew I had come home.

The moon has gone and the dawn is starting to light up the sky at the side of the road. Soon, white families will be on their way: mothers ferrying their darling rosebuds to school, fathers off to work to build up money for the white state. My own family was swept away by a flood of fire.

Yes, I can feel that the time is almost right. My AK-47 was my pillow last night. My mother will be guiding my aim, little Sipho will help me pull the trigger: he was always good with his hands, even at steering his pencil through the minefield of his school exercise books. Uncle Hashe, the horse, who died in police custody after the 1976 uprising, he will give me strength.

My home has been destroyed and now I carry my home with me wherever I am, like a tortoise. I may die. But then we all have to die some time. And I think I am dead already.

3. Claire Miller

We dressed for school in a hurry that morning because we'd overslept – I think there was something wrong with the alarm clock. Mom was fussing because she'd been worried about all the violence in the country and that made her tense. She used to watch all the news bulletins on TV so she knew whenever there had been an attack. Dad didn't think of it unless he couldn't send his men into the locations to build houses and then all he cared about was losing money.

Anyway, Mom was making the sandwiches and packing in the school juices and Tommy still had to have his homework book signed.

Dad stormed into the kitchen, trying to knot his tie, but he kept making the back flap longer than the front. He grabbed his hard hat and satchel and called, 'Come on, kids. Let's go!'

And Mom answered, too angrily, 'But they haven't finished their breakfast yet.' Maybe she had a premonition. Maybe, in her heart of hearts, she knew and was trying to change the course of things to come.

But I believe in fate. The lines are drawn and, however much we try to shift them from their predetermined directions, we are governed by the bars they have created around us: we are the prisoners of the lines of fate. Maybe if Dad had woken earlier, or if Mom had persuaded him to wait until Tommy had finished his cornflakes – a few minutes either way – everything would have been different. But there was no way we could escape our destiny. Dad had a dollop of shaving cream on his ear and Mom wiped it off with her dishcloth at the front door.

Then it was bags and bodies piling into Dad's car. Mom kissed us goodbye and whispered in my ear, asking whether I'd packed in a sanitary towel in case my period started while I was at school. And I said 'Yes', impatiently, because we'd discussed it the night before, and my chief concern was actually whether I'd learned enough to pass my maths test. Mr Brown had threatened to detain anyone who failed his precious test: he's mean. He knew that the big dance was on Friday night and that we needed Friday afternoon to get ready, to have those last-minute appointments with the hairdresser, to fit our dresses for the last time, to buy our brooches and flowers. But he knows his customers, he knows how to turn the screw.

Tommy was grumbling that it was too early and he wanted to go back to bed, and, when Mom brushed down his hair with her fingers, he jerked away. At nine, he was already trying to be independent. He sat, a picture of misery, huddled into the passenger seat in front, holding his school case tightly on his lap, as Dad pulled out of the driveway with Mom waving anxiously at the gate, still in her gown.

I caught a glimpse of a movement in the curtains of the house across the way belonging to Mr Newton. Since his wife left, he'd been spying on us – a lonely man with a crush on Mom – I didn't know if I should warn her; she might have thought I was crazy. Anyway, I didn't want Dad to go across the road and beat him up, which Dad might have done because he was very protective and had a quick temper. I was relieved to see Mom going inside and closing the door as we turned the corner.

Ahead of us on the open road, dusty at this time of year before the rains came, was the school bus, which we only used to catch if Dad was on site out of town and couldn't take us to school.

The radio was playing boring music, and my mind was wandering ahead to the dance and to Gavin who'd finally plucked up the courage to invite me. He'd been keen on me for the whole year, but was very shy. I thought he was cute, even though my friends said he was a nerd, and I accepted his invitation a little too eagerly. But he was so happy I said yes, I don't think he even noticed the blush that rose in my cheeks. The future was bright with possibilities.

Tommy had crawled out of the cocoon of his unhappiness and was looking through the windscreen. He pointed at a man standing next to the road just ahead. 'What's he doing, Claire?'

Something about the way this man held himself made me take special notice: he wasn't one of those poor labourers, cap in hand, waiting for someone to give him a job. He wasn't walking, but just standing, watching the road as if he were hypnotised. The school bus seemed to wake him up. He bent down into the bushes and lifted up what I first thought was a stick or a log, but when he crouched into an attack position, I knew what it was.

'Get down!' I heard myself shrieking,

The school bus was slewing across the road in front of us. I dived over the seat to protect Tommy, somehow, with my own body. That's when I took the bullet in my back. I felt as if an axe had chopped me in half and I went lame.

Some part of me heard Tommy screaming, 'Claire! Claire! Don't die!' All I can remember after that is thinking that no amount of sanitary towels on God's earth would stop the bleeding, nor would I make the maths test or the dance on Friday night.

They told me that Dad, with a bullet in his chest, kept on driving until he got to a petrol station and then he collapsed on the steering wheel. He lay on the hooter and the hysterical noise woke me up. But the pain from my shattered body was so unbearable that I fell unconscious again.

Four children in the school bus were killed and Dad also died. I couldn't attend his funeral because I was in hospital.

'Critical' is how they described me for a long time; I read the newspaper reports when I was well enough. They also called me 'hero' because I saved Tommy's life; I took the bullet that would have blown out his brains. But what can I do with these words? I will never walk again – no more dances. Gavin came to see me once, painfully, and never again and no one can say when Tommy will start talking again.

Mom has started opening her door to Mr Newton, but she doesn't even see the man who stands before her. Her hair turned white overnight. She held up for as long as it took to nurse me back from the dead, then she collapsed mentally. Our family has been destroyed. For what?

I'd like to say that I have no hatred for that red-eyed killer; often you read of survivors who forgive their attackers. But that would be a lie. I hate him with a every fibre left intact in my body. I don't care what drove him, what circumstances in his life under apartheid caused him to be so angry. Nor do I suppose I'll ever find out: he got clean away, melted back into the squatter camps, just one more face in a baying crowd. Whatever his reasons, he has reduced me to a cripple in a wheelchair for the rest of my life. I hate to think what scars he has left in Tommy's mind, what revenge my brother might take when he grows up.

The problem with this country is that you can't dream of a healthy future. You can only have nightmares.

4. The Enemy Within

The wheel of fortune spins for all of us. Someone starts it rolling and, before you know, it's out of control like the tyres of a runaway Hippo and who knows where it will stop and who'll get run over?

They want to play with fire; they will get burned.

If anyone wants to know where I am, just say I've gone fishing.

– Major Tertius du Preez

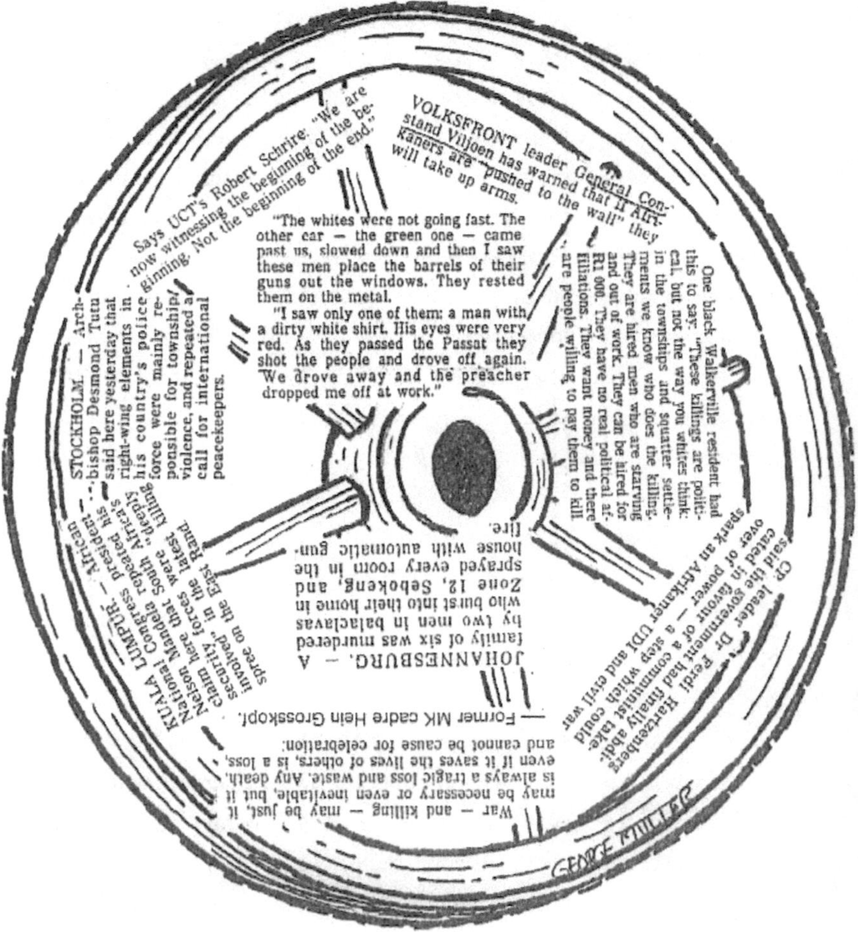

THE BEGINNING

The Vow

'Look at the tables,' he said. His arm made a faltering sweep and fell, like a caged bird trying to fly. 'The owner has arranged them in circles. As if he wanted to damn those who grace his bar. You get the feeling that the owner hates mankind. Do you agree?'

I did not reply.

He continued, as if *he* was the regular, as if *I* needed the explanation. 'Here the lonely come to kill themselves, slowly, drop by drop. For years, they prolong the ecstasy of final death, indulging instead in a series of daily mock deaths, teasing the Black Angel, saying, "Here I am, you have me at last," but then holding out a little while longer. Every day alive is a victory for those who are seeking death.'

'But not just the lonely come here,' I objected. In the semi-darkness, figures sat at tables, alone or with companions. Glasses tinkled, mugs clunked on tabletops, low conversations like our own crept like snails on the mulch of the cigarette haze. In the corner, a game of darts was in progress.

'Oh no,' he said, 'there are those who are sick at heart for other reasons too. And the mentally ill. They all come here to take their slice of this infernal cake. Even the ceiling reflects their turmoil.'

Empty wine bottles hung from the ceiling by their thin necks, black eyes seeking those who had caused their emptiness, like the eyes of dead fish. As you contemplated that rolling sea, it moved, wave upon wave, angles and smooth surfaces. It was a vision of chaos; the eye was disturbed, sight was distorted. I felt sick; I had to look down. I focused again on the man who had come to sit across from me, jolting me out of my daydreams.

'Hello, Colonel,' he said, aware of my scrutiny. 'Can you help me with twenty-nine cents?'

'Do I look as if I can?' I asked, feeling the mockery of his voice like a whip on my face.

He drew his shirt cuff across his nose. He did not speak. I expected him to get up and hobble away, as painfully as he had shuffled up to me, picking me from all the other derelicts in this place. But he remained where he was. He filled his glass, turned the bottle upside-down, allowing the foam to leak from the neck. He watched each drop with an absent intensity as though its passage through the air was of great importance; perhaps he measured oblivion by the number of drops of foam that fell into his glass, perhaps he did not see at all but had become hypnotised by the repetition.

I tended my glass, nursed the contents, held the wine between my hands as if it were as precious as my own blood. Often I have this illusion: that, by drinking, I am putting blood back into my body.

I considered the tables. I preferred to sit in the inner circles: it was safer inside, closer to the bar that was in the centre.

I did not need to get up to receive my wine. A raised finger; the owner knew me well. He served me the red wine I love, dark and warm. I sat, and he brought me what I craved. And I reached into my pockets and dug out coins for him. The relationship between us worked well: we could satisfy each other's needs, Lucien and I.

He was a short, slim man with a thin face and deep brown eyes. He often tied his long hair back in a tail. His sideburns flared down his cheeks; a small beard and moustache surrounded his narrow lips. I thought he had too much hair, as though he were hiding behind it. He did not speak much; his eyes communicated, or his hands: when he was nervous, his hands trembled as he served me, and I feared that he would spill the wine. But he never did. I am certain he would have been apologetic; he would have cleaned up the glass and liquid, and brought me another bottle; he was that kind of man. If anything spilled on me, he would have soaked it up, although the effort of touching me would have drained something from him. He kept his distance, physically and verbally; he was a quiet man, although you could see the pent-up emotion in him. Sometimes you thought he might cry, he looked at you so intensely. And his small hands shook. I notice hands, especially of those who serve me.

'One gets the feeling that the owner hates mankind,' my new companion had said.

I had never gained that impression before, but when I thought about it, it was possible. Who can know what goes on in men's minds?

My companion broke into my thoughts. 'You look ragged, Colonel,' he said. 'I wouldn't expect you to part with money on my behalf.' He smiled. His mocking tone had gone, had been replaced by understanding.

I suddenly felt that he had some reserve of compassion uncontaminated by the world. But that pool was hidden deep under a surface pocked with neglect. His clothes were dirty: a denim jacket with frayed cuffs, greasy jeans, and a shirt that had once been white. His fingernails were bitten so badly that he had drawn blood. A scab between his eyes gave him a third eye; it drew my scrutiny, it was a mark of his degeneration. Yet his hair was cut short, as if a part of him still tried to maintain dignity.

'I was only joking with you,' he said. 'I hope you forgive me. Please don't take it the wrong way.'

I shrugged, uneasy at his intimacy and his inspection. I came to Lucien's bar to merge, to escape, not to be judged.

'You're angry with me, I can see it,' he continued, 'and what can I do? I can't command you to put up with me. Even though I called you Colonel, I can see you're not an army man. I can't order you to listen. I have no authority. Not any more.'

I couldn't tell if he was being wistful or resentful of a time past.

'You see, I'm a very good judge of character. Even though you might say I've let myself go a little, I retain many of my old qualities. You've noticed? You're an observant man.'

The mockery had crept back into his voice. 'So…go if you want. Don't stop to listen to a fool like me.'

'I was sitting here. It's *my* table. *You* intruded.'

'D'you want me to leave?' He pushed his chair back but left his hands resting on the table.

'As you wish.'

He settled again and peered into his glass, looking for the answers there. 'This doesn't help,' he confided. 'Do you think it does?'

'It depends on what you're trying to cure,' I said. My interest was vying with my irritation. 'What?'

He looked at me mournfully, and then suddenly burst out laughing. 'My God,' he gasped. 'You don't cure what ails me. I've turned my back on life…'

He could not continue because of the laughing, which turned into a long racking cough. The sound fell like knotted rope out of his mouth. Some of the patrons turned curiously; others remained with their heads bowed to their glasses, indifferent to my companion's sickness. The coughing was like blows to his body; he winced and tried to dodge, but they got him every time, causing breath and foam to spurt from his mouth. The heaviest punch thrust him on his feet and he stood, half-bent and bobbing, on the ropes but still defiant.

I motioned to Lucien. But he could, or would, not catch my eye. I stood, walked to the bar, and asked for water. His hands were shaking as he gave the glass to me. His eyes were deep discs. For the first time, I felt uneasy in Lucien's presence. He fingered the silver cross that hung from his neck, caressed it as if for comfort when I took the water, as if he were trying to ward off danger. Did my companion's coughing spell remind him of his own mortality, of his own fragile connection to life? I returned to my table and gave the water to the beggar. I was party to a drama that I did not understand.

'Thank you,' the dishevelled man wheezed, and sat again. 'It's my chest,' he explained, sipping noisily. Then he leered, 'Do you think this will save me?' His lips were so thin as to be almost absent; his mouth was a narrow gap in his face.

I was afraid that he would start laughing, and coughing, again.

'Is this pure enough? Will it give me my faith back? And my wife? Do you think it will cure my body? Do you think…?' But the words refused to pass through his throat. He drank, thirstily, as if he had not had water for days or months.

'Listen, Colonel,' he said at last. 'I'm serious about this request. I'm not lying to you. Please help me.' This time desperation had gained a toehold in his voice. 'I need another drink and I have no money. I'm at odds with the world, I'll tell you openly, and it's not easy. I simply need a couple of bob for a drink, just to tide me over for the next little while.'

He picked at the scab on his forehead and added, almost as an afterthought, 'Life is meaningless for me.'

'That's not much of an excuse,' I said. 'Life's not exactly a bed of roses for me either. Who'll buy the next one, and the next?'

His jaws clenched; I could see the muscles knotted below his ears. He gripped his glass so tightly I thought he might crush it and injure himself. And then I would have had to take him to hospital; who else would take him? I did not want him to worm his way into my life.

'I won't ask you for anything else,' he grated. 'I have my pride, you know. I like begging as little as you like beggars. And I don't blame you. They're a pest, a leech, a parasite on good people like you… I'm sorry if I offended you. I'll go now.'

'No, no,' I said hurriedly. I feared that, if I gave in to him, he would come back to bother me, and I can't afford to be generous: I have little enough for myself. On the other hand, if a man is that down, you must try to help. It's only decent. And you never know when the wheel will turn and you'll be begging, and the man you've helped will be your saviour.

I tried to attract Lucien's attention, but he refused to notice me. 'Wait here,' I said to the beggar. 'I'll be back.'

He looked at me with a glance that was a mixture of gratitude and cunning. My leg was acting up again. It's a barometer of trouble:

whenever there's the hint of unease in the air, my leg begins to ache. I limped to the bar. Lucien had his narrow back to me. If he heard my irregular step, he did not turn. I laid my hand on his shoulder, which I should not have done. The next thing I knew – I am not an agile man, my reflexes are not quick, I was hardly aware of the sequence of events – Lucien had me down on the bar and was pricking my throat with the point of a knife. He could have killed me, but he had enough self-control not to plunge the knife in. My scream was strangled in my throat. His eyes were not looking at anything in this world.

'I'm sorry,' he said as he let me go. The wildness withdrew from his face like a cat slinking into an alley. 'I thought you were…the limp… I'm sorry. I'm just a little nervous.'

'Jesus, you gave me a fright!' I complained, holding my hand to my throat. I was amazed that he had not cut me: his speed and force had been tempered by expert control.

Some of the patrons had left at the first sign of trouble; others sat or slumped catatonically, not having noticed. The man whose begging had led me into this attack was unmoved, hunched over the table, seemingly oblivious. I released myself with as much dignity as I could muster and straightened my collar.

'Lucky my pride isn't bound up with my strength,' I said. 'You've publically humiliated me…'

'I didn't mean to. It was a reflex.'

'Why do you ignore me when I call for service?' I asked peevishly. 'After all the years I've been drinking here, this is the first time you haven't come when I've called. What's the matter?'

'Nothing,' he said. 'It's OK.' He waved his arms. 'Don't ask me any more. What d'you want to drink? Anything. It's on the house.'

'My usual,' I answered, slightly mollified, 'and a beer for my friend.'

'Who is your friend?' he demanded. 'Where did you meet him?'

Again the cat began to prowl. The knife gleamed on the counter and I stepped back when Lucien glanced at it.

A black smile darted over his face. 'Don't worry. I'm fine now.'

'How do I know that?' I asked warily. 'You almost cut my throat.'

'But I didn't,' he said, taking out two bottles. 'Please, on me. And no more questions.'

'I don't mind telling you about him,' I offered. 'In fact, there's nothing to tell. He came to my table just now and sat down, uninvited. I hadn't encouraged him – I don't know why he chose me. He asked me to buy him a drink. That's all.'

'Well, you can't afford to support every hobo in town,' he said. 'It's just as well these are for free… I owe it to him, I suppose,' he added cryptically. When he saw my mouth open and my eyebrows lift, he put a finger to his lips. 'No questions,' he cautioned.

I noticed that his other hand did not stray too far from the knife, even when he opened the bottles.

I took the drinks and turned back to my table. But the beggar had gone.

*

Days passed and still the man did not return: I don't know why I expected him to. As was my habit, I arrived at Lucien's bar regularly at eight in the mornings and stayed until five. For a transfusion. No matter what the weather was like, hot or cold, raining or blustery, I spent my days in the bar. Some may whisper behind my back that I've retreated from life, that I took a stand once and was punished, and then threw in the towel. But I don't care what they say. These were peaceful days, and peace was all I wanted: I could rest my leg and avoid the attention of police and thugs. Not being out on the streets meant that I was saving, or at least not being robbed, which amounts to the same thing. And Lucien did not mind how much, or little, I drank.

I had noticed that Lucien was getting more anxious as the days went by. He started when you spoke to him; he always held the knife close. I kept my distance. I would not pry into his life; it was none of my business. Even if sometimes I felt a twitch of curiosity, I stifled it.

One evening, I was looking into my glass at the face of the policeman who had destroyed my leg and my idealism. The bar was empty. Lucien suddenly sat before me, in the place where the tall beggar had sat. I was startled; he had always kept himself aloof from his patrons.

For a while, he said nothing and there was an uneasy silence between us. He shifted in his seat, fiddled with his dishcloth; clearly he was uncomfortable. His eyes were sunken and tired, and he hadn't shaved.

When eventually he spoke, his words burst out like a cork from a bottle: 'You've been coming here a long time. How long is it now?'

I shrugged. 'I don't know exactly. Years… I enjoy coming here.'

'I'm sorry about my reaction the other day,' he said.

'It's OK. Just keep that knife to yourself, and I'll keep coming.' I poured the wine into my glass.

'I want to explain…' he began. 'In case anything happens to me. I want someone to know the story. I've chosen you because he did first. Whatever he tells you, I know you won't judge me too badly. You're loyal…you look like an honourable man.'

I smiled. 'Our mutual acquaintance called me ragged,' I said.

'What d'you mean by acquaintance?' Lucien asked; his voice had developed a harsh edge.

'You seem to know him,' I ventured.

He shook his head, not to deny what I had said, but, it seemed, in pain. He rolled back the sleeves of his black silk shirt and, for the first time, revealed to me his tattooed forearms.

'I suppose you could say these have something to do with it,' he said. 'They are the symbols of my vow…'

'Vow?' I asked.

He was staring dreamily at the door, as if he expected someone to step through to take away the pain. Apart from the tattoos, his forearms were as pale as his face; he saw the sun as little as I.

'To who?'

'To God, myself, whoever would listen, anyone.' He turned on me, suddenly savage. 'Anyone!' he snarled, then dropped his head to spare me the frightening intensity of his eyes. 'Look!' He thrust the tattoos at me. His right arm had an angel, his left a devil. The angel was a naked young girl with enormous wings and a halo; she was lovely. The devil was an old man with a huge erect penis, hooves, and a trident aimed at the girl; a lecherous grin split his face. Both figures were carved with immaculate detail and gaudy colours into Lucien's white arms. As he flexed his hands, they flew, they danced over the wiry muscles and bowed. 'To be safe,' he said, 'I made my vow to both sides.'

'What was the vow?' I asked, spurring him on. He wanted to talk, but he did not know how.

'Revenge for what they did to my family.'

'Did you get your revenge?'

'Yes and no.' He bit the words out of the air.

'What did they do?'

He settled back and stared at the ceiling. He did not bother to conceal the tempting couple on his forearms; they were exposed for anyone who came in to see. Not that they would have meant a thing: they were simply tattoos. They were very beautiful, the fire-red devil and the ivory-coloured girl taunting the viewer with her full breasts, round as apples, smiling innocently as she spread her wings. Lucien touched his fingers to his face, then massaged his neck. I saw that he did not have a drink. Then I realised that I had never seen him drink anything alcoholic: a teetotal barkeeper!

'That day the sky was as blue as burnt metal,' he said. 'There were no clouds to stop the sun. It was a cruel sky.'

As he got used to speaking, as the dam walls of his reserve started to crumble, his words began to flow, the trickle became torrents: I am surprised that, over the years, the emotion he had suppressed had not drowned him. His monologue was a release; I have come to think that it was delivered for its own sake, not for me; I was simply the catalyst to bring it into the open. My nods, my murmurs were the incentives he needed.

'I could see every small detail,' he continued. 'The untarred main road… I knew every stone, every hump. I grew up with them. The trees were wild, not manicured like the ones over here. I was free then. Now I'm in a cage, which I can't deny that I've built for myself. I don't see the sunlight, I don't see the daytime sky. Do you know that I haven't seen blue sky since I opened this bar? I've lived in darkness.' He looked towards the door again; the movement had become a tic.

'I was born in the Republic but my family emigrated north when I was a child. My father thought he could get rich by selling to the natives. He started a general dealers in Mfezi and worked himself to death behind the counter. My mother took over when he died. I was never very close to him, I was too young. In any case, I hardly ever saw him.

'My mother and I raised my sister, Maria. I wasn't only her brother – I was her father as well. She looked up to me in the way that daughters idolise their fathers. And I took my responsibility seriously: that's why I never let any of the other boys get too close to her. She was beautiful, they all desired her. I made it clear that if I caught anyone with her, I'd cut off his balls. I had a temper and they believed me so they stayed clear. She smiled a lot. Her face was dark from the sun and her teeth were brilliantly white. I was also dark then. Now look at me: a ghost. I loved her. I have never loved anyone else. Do you understand?'

I nodded. I admit to a twinge of fear: my stomach was hollow. His eyes had fixed on me like a snake's, blank and dark. I feared he would suddenly realise that he had told me too much. Would I have offended him more by staying to listen or by excusing myself? Yet he obviously needed to talk. So I took another sip of my wine and tried not to be drawn into his empty eyes.

'Can you imagine my mother in the shop? A fat mama with a tongue as sharp as the knives under the counter. The natives respected her because she was honest with them, she never cheated like some shopkeepers.'

He sneered when he spoke about what I presumed was the

competition. 'She always gave them the right change, always measured out the sugar properly... They didn't try to steal, or at least we never caught anyone stealing. Between her and me, we kept them frightened, but I think they liked us. We never mixed with them socially of course – the whites used to stick together – but I think they liked us. Not that they lifted a finger to help when the soldiers came...

'In this dark bar, in the heart of the Republic, it's not easy to imagine how colourful and exciting it was, but I remember it all so well. The natives used to crowd in the street outside the shop. They had nothing better to do. God knows where they got money. Some relative working in the Republic maybe, sending back wages from the mines. I don't know. Their clothes never fitted; everything was too big or too small.'

A smile (of nostalgia or disdain?) touched his mouth and softened his face so that, for an instant, I could see the boy in him, scornful of the sweating faces, the blaring radios, the untied shoes and dancing feet; I know the villages too.

'They had no idea of reality,' he continued. 'They seemed to live in never-never land. It's their shirts I always remember, advertising political parties or football teams or places they could never have been to. The natives were the source of my income, the source of my sister's happiness, that was all. I didn't need them for anything else.

'I have a memory of my sister running through the village with the sun flashing on her silver cross.' Again he reached for the cross resting on his chest and I knew it was the same, deprived for years of the life that had surged through this sullen man's sister, now dark and lacklustre after too much time in the company of the fallen. His nervous fingers did not reach their destination; overcome by a tremendous weight, they dropped.

Unwillingly, I looked at his eyes. They were...dead, ageless, the timeless look of those for whom time no longer matters. The eyes were trained on me and, uncomfortably, I had to look away, anywhere but on those mirrors to an inner decay.

'There were no clouds in the sky when the soldiers came,' he said. 'It was pitilessly hot. They came at midday when the town was closing for lunch. I was standing in the street watching my sister. They came in a jeep, four of them, sweating like pigs. So much sweat, like mirrors. You could see your reflection in their faces.'

His voice had dropped to a whisper and he spoke in a monotone. I had to lean forward to hear him; some of his words were so faint, they were almost lost.

'It was quiet, deathly quiet,' he said. 'All the village noises died: the talking, the radios, even the insects. My sister went to hide behind a twenty-gallon drum; I saw her watching with her big eyes, the eyes of a scared twelve-year-old… What happened next was not real. It was a play where all the actors performed their parts according to a script. The crowd of natives melted away, and the sergeant walked straight to the shop followed by his soldiers. He stopped outside and sent them in… I never knew why he had it in for us. Isn't it strange how hurt leads to hurt? Someone upset him so he took it out on us, and I took it out on…'

Again he glanced at the door, briefly, and then returned his unnerving stare to me. 'Ghosts,' he said. 'They rattle their chains at the doors of your mind. They demand to come in. You can't keep them out: ghosts are everywhere, shaking your brain with their howling. Do you understand?'

I did not. His passionate words and dead eyes were so at odds with each other that I was sure I was listening to the ravings of a madman.

'Yes, I understand,' I said to placate him, but I felt my lower lip quiver as it sometimes does when I'm out in the cold looking for a place to sleep and the chill bores into my bones. 'I understand.'

'We all have our own ghosts, but we're all the ghosts of others,' he said cryptically. 'The play went on while I watched. Even if those men had wanted to act differently, they were not allowed to. But of course they all wanted to do what they did. Bloodlust! Men get so much pleasure from it.

'Three men dragged my mother out of the shop and not one of her customers lifted a finger to help her. There were enough of them but they did nothing. It was *their* country, *their* soldiers, *we* were the white foreigners from the evil Republic, *we* had set up businesses that took the food out of the mouths of the natives, or so they might have believed. Maybe that's why they hated us and sent their soldiers. They didn't remember the charity my mother gave their children when they couldn't afford to buy. She cared; she pretended to be hard, she had to, but she cared. I admit I didn't. But why kill her? And why spare me?

'They hit her on her face with their gun butts so that the blood spurted. They pulled her into the street and dropped her in the dust. The sergeant took his pistol from its holster, smartly, so smartly, following the play script, and shot her in the head. As you see in the movies. No reasons, no chance to defend herself against any crime that she might have stood accused of, not even emotion. It was as callous as the way you'd wipe a cloth over ants in your kitchen.'

I did not interrupt to say that I had no kitchen, even though such inconsequential thoughts entered my head as a protection against the story he was telling. I have also suffered and I've listened to some awful stories. You can't let it all touch you too personally. You have to keep your distance.

'She made no sound,' he went on. 'She was too proud to give them the satisfaction of hearing her plead for her life. Her body lay in the road and the bright, cruel sun burned it. The sunlight engraved the picture on my mind through my eyes. Can eyes see sights like that and still remain as balanced as they were before?'

And, as if he had read my mind, or divined my thoughts through my actions, he said, 'Do you think that my eyes would be calm and gentle after seeing a vision like that? I did nothing to save her because there was nothing I could do. And the natives just stood around and watched. Why weren't their eyes burned out, I want to know? I've often thought about that.' He put a hand over his eyes.

I thought the story had ended and I was wondering what to say, what condolences to offer.

But he sat back in his chair, lowered his head in a reflex movement towards the cross, and continued to speak. 'They found my sister behind the drum and picked her up in their enormous hands. Her screaming unhinged something in me. I saw the sergeant grinning and starting to unloosen the belt of his trousers. I knew what he was going to do. I threw myself at him, a human missile. That's all I remember.

'When I woke up, everyone was gone. The street was empty. The sun blazed down. Everything was so clear, exposed. They had left us lying there like dogs in the dirt. The shop was looted, my mother and sister shot. I don't know why they didn't kill me also. Maybe they wanted me to suffer more. Believe me, it was worse to be alive than dead. I should have died then, too. What right did I have to live when my family was dead? My sister's dress was up around her waist…she was covered in blood down there. All the natives must have seen what he did to her. She was only twelve…'

'I had the impulse to touch him, comfortingly, but I kept control of my hands. I let them drift instead towards my drink. The bottle was empty, another candidate for the decor of the ceiling.

'Let me get you another,' he said.

'I can only afford two a day,' I pointed out.

'It's on me,' he said and went to fetch a bottle. He opened it and poured. 'Thank you for listening,' he said. 'You've been patient with me.'

'It's nothing,' I said graciously. 'I've always felt good coming here. It's the least I can do.'

What unnerved me, and I'll say it again, was the discrepancy between the concern in his voice and the death in his eyes. He seemed to be going through the motions of social etiquette for my benefit even though he felt none of it. Like the soldiers, he had learned his lines and was delivering them because he had to. Except that his delivery was unconvincing; he was a bad actor. Maybe he had no more grief, no pain, nothing.

'I was too ill to attend the burials,' he said. 'I lay with fever for days or weeks and I made my vow to take my revenge on the natives. I was delirious. One minute, I spoke to God, the next to the Devil. Neighbours looked after me. Their boy was a tattoo artist. I asked him to do these pictures. I wanted to have someone from each side with me at all times. This,' he touched the cross, 'this was Maria's. I've worn it all these years.'

He held the thing absently; he rubbed it between his fingers as if it were a magic lamp and out of it would come the spirit of his sister. But he had no need to call her ghost; it haunted him in any case.

'I lived in silence during those days,' he continued, and then smiled. 'I don't speak much now either, do I?'

I shook my head.

'At least I can speak if I want to,' he said. 'Then I couldn't. But my mind was full of these characters. God was the angel with Maria's face and butterfly wings. She used to fly around the room, just out of my reach. She was so beautiful. She settled on the window where the light caught her and sat there for hours while I looked at her. The Devil lived under the floor. He was a dirty old man with a prick so big that he had to hold it in both his hands as he walked. I tried to stomp on him, but he was too clever. Sometimes the people who owned the house came in and found me jumping up and down, screaming. How could I tell them that he was trying to get at Maria and I was trying to save her? Those were my dreams…'

He looked at me with an expression of alarm. 'I'd better shut up or you'll think I'm hopelessly insane,' he said. 'But please understand that I had a fever and I've never seen these images again.'

'You must have been very upset,' I said clumsily.

'One night, when my body was healed, I rode out of town on a donkey. I didn't tell anyone I was going. I just slipped out, like a tramp skipping without paying.'

I raised an eyebrow – I did not appreciate the metaphor – but did not interrupt, and he went on.

'I had my father's revolver that he'd hid under the floorboards of our house, some bullets and food. After a few days' travelling, I got to the border. There were two guards. I shot them both and crossed into the Republic. I came home. But I was an exile, an exile in the country of my birth. After I'd convinced the people at the recruiting office that I wasn't hostile, they accepted me into their army. It was a long time ago.'

'You fought in the war?'

He nodded thoughtfully as though he had to recall the facts from a distant country. In the dim green light of the bar, some customers who'd come in moved slowly as if they were walking under water. There must have been some dry throats; Lucien was neglecting his duties.

'On the north-eastern border,' he said, 'they were fighting with the natives. The "bush war" they called it. They needed all the help they could get. Do you remember?'

I nodded. The bush war had been a national obsession covered luridly by the popular press. Daily we were shown pictures: of our soldiers crouching over rifles and maps, of camouflaged men creeping through head-high grass, of dead terrorists lined up in rows like fish on a beach. Lists of the dead, lists of the missing: it was a disease. I opposed the madness, and look what they did to me.

'They took me,' Lucien said. 'It was perfect. It gave me the chance for revenge...'

'Revenge on who?' I asked. 'Did you expect to meet that sergeant in the bush?'

'I had made my vow to take revenge on the natives. It didn't matter who I killed, how many. The more the better, that was all. I wanted blood. Do you understand?' His fingers clenched the knife as if it were a lifeline. 'There's no heaven, no hell. God doesn't get involved in the affairs of men. I've learned these things. You have to carve your own fate. Neither the girl nor the old man could help me. I carved my own revenge. My vow became a promise to myself not to tire of the job, to keep at it, to wash out the memory with blood.

'Yes,' he sighed. 'I admit. In the safety of this bar, it all sounds a little melodramatic, but out there, in the bush on the border, it was all too real. And I wasn't the only one with scores to settle. The boys had boxes of fingertips, necklaces made from ears: trophies. Don't wince. Grudges real or imagined, fuelled that war. You've heard war stories, I'm sure. I could raise your hair, but I don't want to upset you any more than necessary. I'll stick to essentials. You were never in the army?'

'No,' I said. 'I've always tried to sort things out peacefully.'

'Good, very good,' he replied in a low voice, 'only sometimes you have no choice: you have to face the conflict head-on. To kill the demons that claw in your head, you have to relive the nightmare, again and again, every day. So it was with me. The vow controlled me rather than the other way around; instead of reminding me, it drove me. It became my master. It goaded me with its fork,' he glanced at his forearms, 'and tempted me with its beauty. It made me behave strangely. I had to get rid of my anger and my hatred. I'm telling you this so you can understand the next part of the story. I hope I'm not boring you.'

'Oh no,' I assured him, 'but I think that man wants a drink. He's been trying to attract your attention.'

Lucien looked around worriedly; for a moment, I suspect, he thought it might have been the beggar whom I had come to consider his nemesis.

He buttoned his cuffs, once more imprisoning his relics. 'Excuse me,' he said. 'You will stay for the next chapter, won't you?'

'Of course,' I murmured into my beard, which was a bit wet from wine that I had dribbled. 'I've got nowhere else to go.'

I was fully aware then of the extent of his isolation from the world; he had destroyed all bridges with other people, and now he was uncertain that the flimsy structure he had established with me was strong enough to endure a short parting. He seemed to walk away in a vacuum, as though he was indeed the ghost he had called himself. He glanced over his shoulder as he walked; perhaps he feared that the man with the racking cough and red eyes would return to steal his place at my table. He was away for a very short time.

'We were fighting in the bush,' he began. 'By the way, do you want another bottle? How are you doing?'

'I still have enough,' I said. I did not want to get drunk; if there was trouble, I needed to be in control of myself. My crippled leg is enough of a handicap. It behaves badly when I'm drunk; it has a will of its own. After the security police had finished with me, I was so wrecked they had me walking in two directions at the same time.

'Good,' he said. 'Picture the scene. It's hot, as hot as the day when the soldiers came to my village. We're swimming in our sweat. Every time we open our mouths to drink or speak, insects fly in. Can you understand why I need darkness now? Bright sunlight has taken on dark associations. Only in the dark can I find any lightness in myself.

'We've made a camp in a clearing. We've dug trenches in circles,' he drew concentric circles with his finger in the air, 'around a core of provisions and equipment. Can you believe that we used human flesh to protect guns? But no one thinks of this while we sit in the earth, with the smell of sweat and crap and mouldy rations. You don't forget smell.

'The worst comes from our prisoner of war, not because of the native smell, which is bad enough, but because he's got diarrhoea. He's unconscious in the trench near me, lying in his own shit and vomit. The men hate him, they want him to go away, to be shot, just to disappear and to take the flies with him. Maybe he reminds them how close death really is.

'But the CO needs the native alive for interrogation and he's called a helicopter to fetch him. It lands in the clearing, just beyond the trenches. The first person to get out is the medic. He's tall and blond, just a boy, smiling, I don't know why. I have never forgotten his face…

'At this point, I'm very irritable. The rotors have kicked up a lot of dust and there's grit in my eye. I try to wipe it out, but it's stuck and it hurts. And I'm choking on the smell of shit. Now I don't use that as an excuse for what I did,' he scratched his eye reflectively, 'although it must have played a part.'

He stopped speaking and for a brief moment we were both lost in our own thoughts.

'The sun makes the air vibrate with white heat,' he continued. 'It even sucks in noise. Every muscle in my body is tight, tight enough to snap.' His eyes glazed over in recollection.

'What did you do?' I prompted.

'What did I do?' he repeated, as if he had not heard me clearly. 'The question is if I did anything. My vow had a life of its own: it used my body as a tool. When I lay sick with my nightmares, I never imagined what it would make me do. I keep the tattoos covered now, but I'm stuck with them forever. I've learned that hurt leads to hurt and you've got to take the consequences of what you do. But I'm sure you know it. You have wisdom, I can see. And compassion. That's why I'm speaking to you: I knew you'd understand. I couldn't bear pity, but I crave understanding.'

I nodded and scratched my head doubtfully: compassion had led me astray before.

'They discharged me, dishonourably,' he continued. 'I'd served them well, I'd done their dirty work, and they fired me with a bad reference because of a moment's slip. They trained the parcels of grudges and fears that they recruited, they turned us into their killers. Which is all very well. But when we strayed from their rules, they punished us. Does that make sense to you? I don't regret what I did. Over the years, I've often thought about it; I've examined it from every angle. I've even read books to try to understand myself. I've decided that there's no justice. There's only one rule: hurt leads to hurt. I've banned angels and devils from my life...'

'So,' I prodded, my curiosity fully aroused, 'what happened? You haven't told me.'

'I shot him,' he said, hunching his shoulders.

'The native?'

Lucien's eyes drooped and his head fell on to his chest. 'Yes,' he admitted. Suddenly, he looked drained. All that energy had slipped from him like spilled wine from a discarded bottle; his secret was released.

He pushed his chair away from the table. 'All this talking is difficult,' he said. 'I've told you things that no one else knows. Thank you for listening. I needed to talk. But I'm tired now and it's time to close the bar. Maybe we'll speak again tomorrow, I don't know. I've told you all I can... Have another bottle for the night. It's on the house.'

'If that's what you want,' I responded, 'but you began telling me your story because you wanted understanding, and I feel that you haven't told me the whole story.'

I knew then that I was treading on dangerous ground. The cat began to prowl over his face, the same look I'm sure that greeted the soldiers discussing the native's future on that bright, fateful day.

'Do you think, in the light of what I've told you, I could have avoided shooting that native?' Lucien asked wearily. He stood up, walked to the bar and brought back a bottle for me.

I accepted it, feeling strangely cheap, as if he had bought my services with a few drinks, as if he had simply used me to justify his actions, and now he was packing me off like a used whore. Clutching the bottle and the tatters of my dignity, I limped out, wondering whether I would return. My last vision of Lucien was of the barman leaning on his bar with his head in his hands: a man in torment if ever I have seen one and, believe me, I've seen a few.

*

The full moon was huge in the sky: a great neon sign, lit from the inside. A hot night; I would have trouble sleeping. I sat on a bench overlooking the reservoir. Only some distant traffic noises nibbled at the silence. I was savouring the prospect of opening the bottle that Lucien had given me. Sometimes, unscrewing the top gives as much satisfaction as the drink itself. On such a night, rich and hot, with the comforting feel of the cool glass in one's hand, who could ask for more? All around, the darkness of the place concealed the memory of the glaring day. The water of the reservoir was black; it hid the sins of the city. Above the stone wall on the far side of the water, the moon was rising, unnaturally big. I could almost reach out and touch it. Its light began to bathe the water.

A crunch of gravel disturbed my tranquillity. I supposed it was a late-night walker, a man with dogs. I did not turn, but waited for the intruder to pass. However, the footsteps came towards me. I tensed with the sudden vulnerability of a potential victim and transferred my grip on the bottle so that I held it like a club. What a waste of good wine, I thought, although I did not expect to land a blow: I am far too old and slow. An agile assailant could have cut me down before I even began the upswing. A man my age shouldn't have to live like this! Still I did not turn. Hopefully they'll ignore an old tramp, I thought.

The newcomer cleared his throat. 'Hello, Colonel,' he said, and I lifted my bottle in fright. Some of Lucien's fear of the man had been transferred to me.

'Don't be afraid. I won't hurt you, old man.'

'How did you find me here?' I asked. I was flabbergasted; he was the last person I expected to see.

'I followed you from the bar,' he said. 'I've been walking up and down, wondering whether to come and talk to you. I need your help.'

'Again?' I asked sarcastically. 'The last time you asked for help, you didn't even have the decency to wait for it. Why should I help you?'

'He recognised me,' the man said, more to himself than to me, 'and he was very nervous. I couldn't stay.'

'He nearly stuck his knife into my throat, that's how nervous he was,' I agreed.

'Do you mind if I sit down?'

'I don't want to be unkind, but you have a habit of butting in,' I said irritably. Now that the fear had gone, I was angry. I don't ask for much out of life, but I do like a bit of peace and quiet. My privacy had been invaded far too often recently. 'You're very insistent,' I conceded at last. 'Sit if you want.'

'Thank you,' he said. 'We are gentlemen of the road. If we're unkind to each other, who'll take care of us? We should support each other. We have no one else.'

'Don't lecture me, sir,' I said. 'I've been living like this for long enough to know what I need. Besides, I've had the kindness of that barman. He's taken care of me for more years than I care to remember.'

The man winced. I saw his face twitch in the moonlight.

'I'm sorry, but the help I want is simply an ear. Please listen to what I have to say. I don't want advice; I've already chosen my course of action. I just want you to understand why I'm going to do what I've planned. I just want to explain. Will you listen?'

'Why me?'

'Because you have compassion. And understanding. I feel that I can talk and you'll give me a fair hearing.'

'Do you want me to be your judge?'

'If you choose to see it like that.'

'I choose nothing, sir. You've sought me out. Twice.'

'All right, then. You be my judge. But I warn you that whatever you decide, whether you judge me moral or not, I'll do what I have to.'

'I'm not a policeman. I can't stop you. Tell me, but I'm not responsible for your behaviour. I suppose it's got to do with Lucien.' I cannot deny that I was intrigued by this strange affair. By chance, I had become the ear of two people who could not talk to each other.

He started when I mentioned Lucien. 'Why d'you suppose that?' he asked suspiciously.

'Because you've mentioned him,' I said. Because the two of you are obsessed with each other, I might have added.

'Yes, you're right. It has got to do with him.' He fidgeted as he sat beside me, shuffling his feet in the gravel. 'Listen, Colonel,' he began, 'I hate begging, as you know, but I see you have a bottle there, and I wondered…I wondered if I might have a little drop. Only a small one. Would you mind? My throat is so dry.'

I unscrewed the top and took a great swig myself. It was as smooth as silk, warm as blood; the sensation under the full moon was delicious. I would have liked to keep it to myself. But I was getting paid, so to speak, by the story. For which the wine itself was payment. There was a bond between the three of us; we were united by the wine, it was a communion of the fallen. I passed the bottle to my companion and he drank deeply. I did not rebuke him for taking more than the drop he had asked for; I hadn't expected him to behave like a saint. He handed the bottle back a shade reluctantly, and wiped his mouth with the back of his hand.

'It's good stuff,' he said. 'Good old Lucien.'

'Do you know him well?' I pressed, considering that I had earned the right to ask. I was not afraid of him in the way that I feared Lucien.

'I don't know him at all,' he said, 'which is why killing him will be so much easier.' He laughed as I recoiled. 'Thank God it's warm tonight. You don't know what cold air does to my chest. Don't be afraid of me, old man. I'm not going to hurt you. You're my judge, not my victim. If I wanted to harm you, I could have done so already, and then taken the wine for myself. I'm not an indiscriminate killer. In fact, I've never killed anyone before in my life.'

'But you were in the war,' I suggested.

'I was a medic,' he said, confirming what I'd already guessed. 'My job was to save, not to take, life: I was an idealist then. When I joined up, I wanted to serve my country and my fellow man. I was a staunch Republican. I also wanted to heal the wounded.'

'Wounded natives too?' I asked caustically.

'Yes,' he said, seemingly oblivious to my barb. 'In war, the medics are a cosmetic touch, intended to put a mask of civilisation onto a brutal face. If a native needed medical care, it was my duty to supply it.'

'How very noble of you.'

'One night,' he went on, ignoring my sarcasm, 'I had a terrifying vision of death. It appeared to be an omen, a warning that I was in danger. I was sitting next to a lake, just as we're sitting now, and the dark water was being whipped up by a desolate wind which assaulted the palm trees and made them ragged. I was overcome by a feeling of utter loneliness in that place away from home, away from my wife who I'd left to follow my ideal. I seemed to be looking into the next world.

'Now, some people talk of white light and tunnels and so on, but to me, then, death was a dark hole occupied by a howling black wind. It seems right that, tonight, the night before I close the circle on my idealism, I should be sitting again before a dark lake. What horrors does that black water hide? What secrets has it swallowed?

'I used to believe in God and Republic. I used to believe that God worked hand-in-glove with us, that He was helping us win the holy war against the natives.' He snorted in contempt. 'Forget about that, my friend. Never trust anyone who claims to have God on his side – he's only trying to justify murder. There were no angels flying around in those trenches. Not bloody likely.'

He picked at the sore between his eyes. His additional sight, his third eye, was a festering wound on his forehead; what warped insight did it give? I was not to judge; I had told him so. Each man has his own systems and beliefs. Who can say what is right and what is wrong for others? I had been punished for opposing the war: that was my choice. We have to take the consequences of our choices.

'The day after I had my vision, they sent me into the bush to fetch a native prisoner,' he continued. 'He was sick or injured, they said, and I had to get him back alive. Another routine mercy mission. As for my vision, it was day, bright. I was invulnerable. The bush was as beautiful and treacherous as ever, but no one shot at us and we landed without incident at the camp.'

I could see that he was reliving the actual experience in his mind as he spoke; it was not simply a memory.

'The man was in a trench, unconscious. He was covered in shit and flies. The soldiers were all hoping he would die. Given half a chance, they would have shot him and cut him up and sent the pieces home to their girlfriends. That's what the war did to them. That's how I know that God has deserted the Republic. If they could behave like this to His creatures in His name, and He allowed them to, then He was either in league with the Devil or He had gone.' The beggar chuckled bitterly. 'Or He had never existed in the first place.

'I needed water to wash the native so that I could work on him. He stank so much, I couldn't even get close. I had to get a drip in his arm, he was so dehydrated.

'A soldier was staring at me from the trench. At first I thought he wanted to help. I called him over. I remember his eyes, as if he was dead. I've seen corpses with eyes like that. He was staring in a way no one has ever looked at me before: without any expression, he was dead, that's all I can say.'

My companion's breathing was irregular now, as he became more excited. 'The soldier didn't move when I called him. He just stood there looking at me. My mistake…my mistake…' his voice was breaking, 'was not recognising that you don't tamper with the dead. I wanted to impose my will on him – I was a corporal, I had the authority. I told him to get a bucket of water and to wash the prisoner. Water was scarce, they had to dig for it. I knew that, but I had to save the man's life. When the soldier didn't move, I insisted: the native was dying and I couldn't work on him like that…

'Please, another drop,' he implored. 'My throat is crying for more.'

I passed the bottle immediately. He threw his head back and poured the wine down his gullet. He wiped his mouth and kept the bottle in his lap.

'He had tattoos on his arms,' my friend said. 'I saw those tattoos when he shot me.'

The beggar turned to see if I had taken in what he had said. It was a dramatic pause, for effect. I can imagine him dining out on this story (whereas Lucien kept it bottled up), and pausing every time at this point for the shock value. I was shocked. For a moment, considering the company I had been keeping, I felt surrounded by the living dead.

'He fired six shots, I learned later. Four hit me: two in my right arm, one in my chest, and one in my leg. The other two killed the native. Poor bastard. It was probably his best option anyway. Lucien did him a favour, saving him from interrogation.

'I was conscious throughout. I saw Lucien drop the gun and walk off into the bush. Someone chased after him. I lay on my back telling them how to put the drip in my arm. But they were clumsy and kept missing the vein. Their hands were trained to kill not to save. Eventually they got me on the chopper and took me back to town. That's my story.'

'And your injuries?' I asked. 'How badly were you hurt?'

'I'm a fucking medical dictionary,' he said. 'This arm's shorter than the other. Look,' he held his arms together, 'but what the hell? The bullet in my chest played havoc with my lungs. Tthat's why I cough – it's the scar tissue. They warned me that I might get TB but what can I do? I've turned my back on society: there's no more meaning for me. I live out in the open, like you, and I take my chances. My left foot is withered where the muscles have atrophied because the nerves are damaged. I get neuralgia. In the winter, I have terrible pain. I've got puncture marks all over my body…' His voice faded and he drank again.

I have a picture of him in my mind, forlorn, bitter, about to perpetuate the spiral of harm, drinking away the pain.

Lucien did not drink; he kept his pain to himself, nurtured it, nourished it, let it feed off him year after year. He helped his patrons destroy themselves while they were relieving their suffering; Lucien simply let his distress chew at him like a welcome parasite. Despite his skill with a knife, I wondered how strongly he would resist an assassination attempt; the beggar was, after all, an answer to a lifetime of grief and guilt. For all the years I had known him, the silent barman had been waiting for delivery from his life. His vow had ultimately turned a full circle of its own; now he could get revenge on himself for surviving his mother and sister. Two circles were due to be completed. in the morning.

'I was paid out for my adventure,' the beggar said to me, 'but how can you compensate someone for disillusion? How can you pay for lost dreams? Because, bad as my physical injuries were, it was my loss of faith in the Republic, its fight, and my fellow man that has led me to this.

'I was filled with fear. I used to wake up at night in terror. Everything was terrifying: the darkness, the trees, the shadows of people walking past. And in the daylight, the heat was as bad: the shimmering mirages…'

He shook his head. 'When I got out of hospital, I was crazy. My irrational rages gave way to attacks of panic. Bursts of anger, like the explosions from the gun, fell into bottomless lakes of desolation, and sank.

'My wife tried to nurse me. Once I chased her through the house, hitting her on the head with my fists. I don't even know why I did it. Of course she left me. Who could live with a man like that? My rages and fears… I was dangerous. I'm glad she left: I might have killed her.

'My life was…is…meaningless. I've told you that. Except for one thing: to find him. It was my only reason to wake up in the morning.'

He slammed the bottle against the side of the bench and it shattered. 'Well, now I've found him and I can take my revenge. I vowed to kill the bastard who destroyed my life. Tomorrow I will fulfil that obligation.' He waved the jagged bottle neck like a dagger.

The moon had risen so that it was a tight ball, a heavenly eye, watching.

'He's even given me the weapon. So what do you say? How do you judge me?'

I did not answer. What could I say? I had a fleeting worry that, now he had told me, he would have to eliminate the witness.

TRAMP STABBED DEAD AT RESERVOIR, the headline would read and the story would detail how the corpse had been found with terrible wounds in a pool of blood amid the glass of a broken bottle.

But he no longer needed my approval. Nor did he fear my

testimony. He had only needed to talk so that he could make his story real, he who had been surrounded by death, but only now was seriously committed to administering it.

'There is no morality in this world,' he said, and it was uncanny how his words echoed Lucien's, two philosophers arriving at the same conclusion. 'There is no universal justice. You have to fight for your own justice…' He was drumming the fingers of his free hand on the bench. 'Do you understand?'

'But what will happen to me?' I wanted to ask. 'Where will I spend my days now? Where will I be safe from the sun? I, too, am a creature of darkness. My old eyes are affected by bright light, my fish-pale skin is no longer used to heat. If you kill Lucien and they shut the bar, what will I do? The old find it hard to change habits, even old tramps. That haunted man who destroyed so many lives had ironically kept me alive.'

But I remained silent, looking out over the dark water.

After a while, he got up. He placed a hand on my shoulder. 'Thank you for listening,' he said, 'and for sharing your wine with me.' Then he walked away, unsteadily, limping into the night.

Dreaming of Alice

The monkey used to sit in the window opposite and masturbate. Can you imagine anything more ridiculous than watching a monkey watching you and jerking off?

– What kind of monkey was it?

I don't know. A baboon, maybe. One of those from the hills around Cape Town. The neighbours must have picked him up on a camping trip and brought him home. They kept him on a chain. He was tied around his neck. I remember the grimace on his face, teeth bared, the sheen on his coat and his bony fingers as he played with himself. I felt sorry for him.

My cousin Alice used to tease him. I think that's why he decided to come to our house when he escaped. Maybe he wanted to get even with her, maybe he wanted to rape her – if an ape can formulate the idea of revenge.

– How did he escape if he had a chain around his neck?

I don't know. I've never known. Maybe he had some sort of native intelligence, a cunning born of desperation to be free. I mean, here you have an intelligent creature – although I didn't understand at the time, I was only fourteen, and it was a very different scientific era – just a few genetic letters away from ourselves.

Can you imagine this ape man – for he was very much a man as I've said – (laughs self-consciously) being plucked from his tribe where he was the king, head of the family, looking after his wife and kids, and being taken like a slave to a tiny house where they imprisoned him with a chain around his neck?

– But weren't there laws against keeping wild animals in captivity? Why didn't the authorities come and take him away and put him in a zoo?

Or perhaps he could not have been put back in the wild and survived after living with humans?

Laws…that's a good question. I don't think anyone in those days even thought about laws. The people next door just went out for a picnic one day and an ape jumped on their car to scrounge for food and they grabbed him and covered him in a towel to stop him from biting them and brought him home as they might have picked up a stray dog. Nobody cared about laws.

So, as I've said, this ape used to sit in the window and fantasise about Alice, or being back with his wife in the bush, and he would relieve his frustration in full view of us kids.

— Did you consider the neighbourhood to be well-educated, A-B income level?

There was nothing A or B about it. (She laughs sourly.) If you want to be charitable, you might have given it an F. They, we, were working-class people. The men worked on the railways, in the police force, in the public sector. The government gave them jobs which, these days, the black government gives to the blacks. It's still apartheid, just in reverse. Now it's OK because it's being done by the 'legitimate' people of South Africa, the indigenous ones…

My mother was a very vain woman. My father had left when I was about ten. He'd had enough of her, I suppose, and he just walked out one day and never came back.

My mother remarried. That second husband, my stepfather, used to drink and then he'd swear at me, and sometimes hit me. He used to beat me randomly. I would always position myself close to a door so I could escape.

Even these days, I never sit in a corner where there's no escape.

— That's terrible. Why did he behave like that?

I think he got a perverse pleasure out of it. It wasn't that I was naughty. Of course, we went to clubs and smoked, but what was it to him? Maybe it was a power trip for someone who was otherwise so powerless. I hardly knew the beast.

Thank God she kicked him out – he went with his tail between his legs – although (wry grin) it wasn't because of me. I think it was because he drank all their money away and she wouldn't stand for it.

She wouldn't try to protect me. She was too involved in her own life, her own fun, caskets of wine with the neighbours, visiting the shops to look at the dresses, going to the dances at the club on Saturday nights. (She wipes away a tear.)

Sorry, I'm digressing. You came to ask me about the time the apeman somehow managed to break the shackles and free himself from his enslavement in the house of bondage next door.

He might have worked out how to pick the lock, or the mechanism by which the chain enslaved him. Or perhaps the neighbours, one day, were negligent and untied his noose, maybe a touch of kindness to let him have a bit of freedom to roam around his prison for a few hours. And he got out.

When he came to our place to find Alice, he was disappointed. She wasn't there. He came early in the morning just as I was waking up. My mother must have left a window unlocked because I opened my eyes and there he was – a huge black shape in the doorway, leering at me with his yellow eyes, his velvet coat glistening in the light from the kitchen.

I remember his fangs as he opened his mouth to grin at me, saying, 'I've got you now, my little one. I've been trapped in the house of the humans for so long but now I'm out and you're my prisoner. I've been so sexually frustrated, thinking about my fellow apes in the bush where I come from, so frustrated that I've had to wank in the window while fantasising about doing unmentionable things to you and your cousin. Well, now I'm out and here I am. You're at my mercy and what are you going to do about it?'

A dog would have stayed at home and cowered under the table, a cat might have gone aprowling, but this monster needed revenge for the ignominy he'd endured.

How do you describe the absolute terror when you're confronted by any stranger in your home, let alone such a monster?

He stood there, growling at me, his lips pulled back, exposing his massive teeth, spit falling, a rank stink coming off him. The growling began in his throat: of expectation, warning, lust.

I lay in bed, frozen in horror, mesmerised, overcome by the total insanity of this confrontation.

Then I screamed for my mother, although I'd never had much support from her previously, but in my panic, I even called for *her*.

And, as I did so, he leapt at me, propelled by spring-powered hind legs. I smelled his dirty breath, was transfixed by his yellow stare, splashes of his spit arced towards me. His hairy arms reached out to embrace me.

And from some hidden place in my genetic memory, the solution existed. In a reflex action, I was out of the bed and had whipped my blanket over the flailing limbs and maddened eyes. As the ape screamed in rage, tangling with the bedclothes, I was out of the room and had slammed the door shut.

'Edith!' I yelled, for that's what I called her, and she never objected, which is why sometimes I thought maybe she wasn't even my mother, but had adopted me. 'Edith!'

She came out from her bedroom, breasts flabby inside her nightie, bleary-eyed, scolding me. 'What is it with you?'

I can't remember if those were the exact words used but I'm taking a bit of licence here: it was over forty years ago. That was the kind of tone she'd use.

'It's the monkey,' I said.

'What monkey! What bloody monkey!'

'From the neighbours. It's in my room!'

'You're dreaming. You're having a nightmare. Go back to bed.'

But my hysteria must have penetrated the mists of her sleep.

'That monkey?' she said incredulously. 'The one in the window?'

'Yes, that one.'

'I knew they shouldn't have kept it in their house. I told them to get rid of it. How did it get into our house?'

As if it were my fault. As if I had let it in.

'Call the police,' she hissed.

– *Hissed?*

Yes. She'd hiss in a crisis, when she was stressed.

The number was probably on the wall next to the phone. It was a hell of a thing. A police van came roaring up with a constable and his dog. The pair burst out, up the front path, into the house.

He was a tall man, rakishly handsome (a small giggle). He had on his blue uniform, brown shoes and police hat, I seem to remember. His name was on a tag: Andries Lourens.

'*'n aap?*' Konstable Lourens said incredulously. 'A monkey? Here? In Goodwood?' He pulled his revolver from its holster. '*Kom*, Shannon,' he said and the dog trotted proudly next to him: you could see the love between them; the German shepherd and his best friend, Konstable Lourens.

'*Waar's die aap?*' he barked. 'Where is it?'

Dumbly, overawed by the cavalry in our humble house, I led them to my room while my mother stood in the hallway in her dressing gown. I realised I'd been scratched on the face, but luckily that was all, and I had on my shorty pyjamas.

The growls and thumps that came from behind that door were fearsome. I dared not go too close. In fact, I could not even speak. I just pointed. It could have been a scene from a horror movie with the evil spirit, the poltergeist, screaming its anger and hatred from inside the room, trapped in the bedsheets, knowing that insurmountable force was being mounted outside and that it was going to be a sitting target in there.

'Shoot him!' my mother urged.

'*Nee, mevrou,*' Lourens replied as calmly as he could. 'I can't risk the bullets missing. Maybe they'll go through the walls and hit someone walking past. No, I can't risk it.'

He opened the door just a crack and then closed it again smartly as something whacked against it. His breathing rate increased dramatically and his eyes were wide. '*Dit is 'n aap,*' he said in bemusement. 'A monkey…'

Then he made a split-second decision. He bent down and whispered to Shannon. He ran his fingers through the dog's coat, the soft touch of a lover sending his best friend into extreme danger. You could see a flash of anxiety screw up his eyes for an instant before his professional mask reasserted itself.

'Go, Shannon, *vang hom*!' he said. 'Catch him!' And he let the dog into the room.

I know he loved that dog. I could see it in the way he kept on touching him, how he kneaded the animal's hair and looked into his eyes. But, at the end of the day, they were professionals. They had a job to do. Lourens knew how dangerous it was, but he had no choice. He sent the dog into battle, not knowing if he would ever see his mate alive again.

I dwell on this because I lost a dog of my own recently. A little one who had such a complex personality she was like my child. She studied me and listened to my conversations, to the nuances of my voice, and cuddled me when I was lonely. She couldn't get enough of my touch. She would lie on her back and drink in the feel of my hands on her stomach. How unlike Shannon was my Rosie. He was a wolf, she a flower. She had a remarkable ability to stand on her hind legs like a meercat and then walk, especially when she was asking for food. Time took her away from me. I miss her so badly…

But I digress again. Is this story about monkeys and humans or dogs and humans? Is it about how we take animals into our homes and hearts and how we treat them?

Thank God I didn't see what went on in that room. The noise was terrible. It was a mixture of the most ferocious barking and pitiful squealing, of angry thumping as if something were being grabbed by the scruff of its neck and smashed against a wall until that wall (made only of board) was in danger of breaking.

Where will I sleep, I thought, if my room is smashed to pieces?

I didn't consider the life-and-death struggle involving two sentient beings; I was too young to consider such things. I was only worried about myself.

The battle was apocalyptic: two mighty adversaries in a closed arena, fighting to the death, on the stage of my bed. The noise rose up, filled the house with blood.

The policeman's eyes were wet as he contemplated opening the door to find the corpse of his beloved friend, throat ripped open by the hideous fangs of that primeval man, drained of blood, tongue hanging out of a bloodstained mouth between razor teeth, now useless.

And yet, when the noise was over and the door opened (I didn't look at what they found inside), I heard Konstable Lourens utter a sigh and say, 'Good boy, Shannon. *Kom, my hond.* Come here, my dog. Are you sore?'

This was greeted by a puppy-like yelp.

Someone removed the body of the man of the forest, who would wank no more while dreaming of Alice.

Out of the corner of my eye – all right, I admit, I was compelled to look – I saw the rag doll being carried out by the policeman and the contrite neighbour, who had come to recover his pet but who managed only to salvage its corpse, its long hair matted by blood, its yellowed teeth snarling impotently in a sad, savage face.

They flung the lifeless thing into the back of Lourens's van – all flopping arms and legs – and the dishevelled owner climbed into the cabin so he could explain himself down at the station. He was small and mouse-like with untidy hair and dressed in shorts and thongs. He smelled of an alcoholic drink, even so early in the morning, and tears rolled down his cheeks. I assume he loved his ape as much as Lourens loved his dog.

I didn't think this at the time, but it occurs to me now whether we should see it as slavery that a man can own another man, no matter how wild that man is.

The excitement had attracted a gaggle of onlookers who lined the pavement dressed in their gowns and slippers and curlers, and some early commuters sporting safari suits and briefcases.

'What's going on?' said Aunt Someone – I don't recall her name – who lived across the road. 'It's a dead monkey! In our street!'

'Yes,' my mother trilled: she was now the hero, the centre of attention, even though she'd done nothing, not even come up in defence of the monkey while he sat in the neighbour's window: he wouldn't have wanked at her. But now, just because the excitement happened in her house, she could crow. She didn't fight him off, nor clean up the room afterwards.

No, I had to, and what a filthy mess it was. The poor monkey, in his death throes, had shat all over the room: blood and shit, on the walls, on the floor, on my bed.

My sheets and blanket were covered in bodily fluids – red and green and yellow – and clumps of torn-off hair from both antagonists. I had to wash my bedding. I'd rather have thrown it all away, but we didn't have the money to buy new sheets and blankets – my mother spent it all on booze – and I had to sleep under a towel until they dried. My bedroom stank.

I couldn't go to school that day because of the cleaning – we didn't have a maid and my mother didn't help – and because the police returned to ask me what had happened.

I had to get a rabies shot at the hospital.

A reporter came from the local newspaper. He wrote the story and, thank goodness, he cast me as the hero. I forget his name – it wasn't on the article. I still have the clipping. I brought along a copy for you. Here it is…'

– *Can I keep it?*

Yes, of course.

– *Thank you.*

That reporter could see the whole situation, and that made me want to become a writer. It was then, in my childish way, that I realised how to get my ideas out to the world. Beforehand, they were bottled up in my head. Oh, I could tell Alice, but that's as far as it went.

Alice was one of the first to come over: it was the bush telegraph, as fast in its day as Twitter is now. She was crying. She also had a soft spot for that crazy animal with his laughing fangs, who was as real to us as any human.

You're looking quizzical. Well, it's true. When you looked into his eyes, through the window, you saw a being that was thinking, scheming, plotting; there was an intelligence, a brain as active as that of any human, and, in the part of the world in which we were living, possibly more so.

You see it in all animals, but, in that prehistoric man, it was highly developed. It was also there, but less so, in my darling little Rosie. It's why I don't eat animals. I can't eat anything that dreams (long pause)…

– Go on.

No, that's enough for today. I'm tired. I've run out of words, which you may think is unusual for me, but it's true.

Maybe we can continue tomorrow or the next day, after my treatment.

– I respect that. I would like to discuss next your move to Australia and your life leading up to your great work…

Which one (mischievously)? Aren't they all great?

– You know what I mean: Dreaming of Alice, your breakthrough novel.

Ah yes, inspired by my experience with the apeman. We'll get there …(stands up with difficulty)…I'm not dead yet.

– Just one more question for this session, if you don't mind. What happened to Alice? The real Alice.

Ah, my beloved cousin. Do you really need to know?

– Yes, it'll fill in some gaps in the biography.

She died, just as in the book, but not in the way I fictionalised her death. In the book, she died of cancer soon after, as you'll recall, but in real life, this life, my life, she succumbed to guilt and grief.

You don't believe me, do you? How can a teenage girl grieve for an ape? But it was obvious to me. She never said it out loud, but I knew it. She blamed herself for what happened.

After Shannon took the apeman's soul, Alice was never the same again. I could see her withering away before my eyes, day by day, until she just drifted off and she was gone.

Is that too melodramatic? I don't care. That's the way I see it.

When I wrote the book, I thought it too unrealistic to ascribe her death to such a fairy tale, although the way trends in fiction have gone in the interim, it might have been a better story. Anyway, it's done.

– I see.

And now, if you don't mind, I'll see you out. I need to rest. Thank you for coming to visit. I hope you can make sense of what I've told you.

Until next time.

Acknowledgements

Some of these stories have been previously published or broadcast:
'A Day in the Life': *Staffrider*
'At Play': *Forces Favourites*
'Crossroads': *The Vita Anthology of New South African Short Fiction*
'Outside Intervention': *Sesame*
'Water Money': *Staffrider*
'Fountains': BBC World Service, *Contrast*
'Dog Training': BBC World Service, *Staffrider*

Thanks

Yvonne for your advice and encouragement.

Stephen Matthews for your faith in my work.

Ian Chung for your guidance.

Simon Bosch for your patience and design wizardry.

Louise Gubb for the use of your photograph, *Guguletu 1985*,
on the cover.

George Muller for the Wagon Wheel drawing in 'Gone Fishing'.